RED PRISONER

"Come on," Rockson yelled at his big friend, Archer. "Fast!" The two men took off across the open field like jackrabbits pursued by a fox. They had gone about thirty feet when the Doomsday Warrior heard a sound. From above? They both dove to the ground as a large rope net dropped down from the trees.

The net hit Archer, tangling his arms and legs. He fell over on his side, roaring like a wild beast. Rock felt the net fall over his back, and he shot forward wriggling, avoiding entanglement. He reached the edge of it and came to his knees, pulling his .12 gauge shotpistol up ready to fire.

"Please don't try that," a cold voice said. Rock looked behind him. A Russian officer, a captain with a big red star on his brown cap, was holding a 9mm Special Service revolver aimed right between Rock's blue and violet eyes. On each side of the officer were nearly ten regulars, their Kalashnikovs pointed at the crouching American.

EXCITING ADVENTURES FROM ZEBRA

DOOMSDAY WARRIOR (1356, $2.95)
By Ryder Stacy
Ravaged by the nuclear devastation of World War III, America is now a brutalized Russian colony. But led by a unique soldier of survival, Ted Rockson, a federation of secret American Free Cities rises up to fight the hated conqueror!

DOOMSDAY WARRIOR #2: RED AMERICA (1419, $2.50)
by Ryder Stacy
Rockson must carry out his war of independence in a ravaged landscape of radioactive hot zones crawling with a deadly new race of beings, "the glowers." In this living hell, Rockson is the one man feared by the Russian tyrants!

DOOMSDAY WARRIOR #3:
THE LAST AMERICAN (1489, $2.50)
By Ryder Stacy
A century after the defeat of America, Rockson must battle the deadly Russian KGB, which plans to destroy the fledgling American rebellion by incinerating its leadership in one fell nuclear swoop!

THE WARLORD (1189, $3.50)
by Jason Frost
The world's gone mad with disruption. Isolated from help, the survivors face a state in which law is a memory and violence is the rule. Only one man is fit to lead the people, a man raised among the Indians and trained by the Marines. He is Erik Ravensmith, THE WARLORD—a deadly adversary and a hero of our times.

THE WARLORD #2: THE CUTTHROAT (1308, $2.50)
by Jason Frost
Though death sails the Sea of Los Angeles, there is only one man who will fight to save what is left of California's ravaged paradise. His name is THE WARLORD—and he won't stop until the job is done!

THE WARLORD #3: BADLAND (1437, $2.50)
by Jason Frost
His son has been kidnapped by his worst enemy and THE WARLORD must fight a pack of killers to free him. Getting close enough to grab the boy will be nearly impossible—but then so is living in this tortured world!

Available wherever paperbacks are sold, or order direct from the Publisher. Send cover price plus 50¢ per copy for mailing and handling to Zebra Books, 475 Park Avenue South, New York, N.Y. 10016. DO NOT SEND CASH.

DOOMSDAY WARRIOR #4

BLOODY AMERICA

BY RYDER STACY

ZEBRA BOOKS
KENSINGTON PUBLISHING CORP.

ZEBRA BOOKS

are published by

Kensington Publishing Corp.
475 Park Avenue South
New York, N.Y. 10016

First printing: March 1985

Printed in the United States of America

the world's population. The Russians, who were able to get off many more of their missiles in a first strike, were victorious over the United States. Now, in control of virtually the entire world, except for China, they ruthlessly rule The People's World Socialists Republic.

PLACE: Atomic bombs exploded all over the planet, but primarily in the United States. The U.S. lost one hundred million people within one hour of the attack. Another seventy-five million died within a year. The Russians immediately moved in with massive transports of troops and weapons and quickly took control of much of the country. They built forty fortresses in vital parts of the U.S., huge military complexes from which they sent out search and destroy units of tanks and helicopters, and radiation-suited troops to extinguish the still-burning embers of resistance.

The Russians use the American citizens as slave labor, forcing them to grow crops and work in factories. The Russian high command lives in luxury, the officers having taken the best housing in the remaining cities. The American workers must make do in shabby shanty towns around the fortress complexes. Thirty-five million Americans are directly under the Red rule. Sullen and docile, they carry out their Russian masters' orders, but underneath they hate them. They pray for the day when the legendary Ted Rockson, "The Ultimate American," will come with the freefighters of the hidden cities and release them from their bondage.

ENVIRONMENT: The great number of bombs set off altered the earth's axis. The polar caps began melting, and the forested regions turned to desert. The world was slowly warming, the higher amount of CO_2 in the air creating a greenhouse effect. Lakes, rivers, and streams have dried up in many places. The ecosystem had been almost dealt a deathblow from the war. Ninety percent of the earth's species of plants and animals are now extinct.

The East Coast of the United States is still extremely radioactive. Vast, bare plains stretch hundreds of miles in New York, Connecticut, New Jersey, and Pennsylvania, upon which nothing grows. At the edges of these "hot" zones are forests of mutated bushes and trees covered with thorns and rock-hard bark. Parts of the Midwest were spared as the Russians had plans for eventually using the farmland to grow crops for their own clamoring masses back home. But the soil was now too radioactive for anything but weeds. American slave labor was taken out by the truckload to work, turning the soil in the "medium hot" zones—meaning death within a year from handling the rocks and topsoil still hot enough to send a geiger counter needle off the edge.

The far West had been hit hard. Colorado was spared, mostly because of some bad aiming, but, further on, in Utah, Nevada, California, there had been heavy damage. The area is now a misty, unknown land. Nothing is thought to even live there. Volcanos and earthquakes have become common, and much of the Northwest has been turned into a nightmare of craters, some miles wide.

The South was hit in a haphazard fashion, as if the Russians hadn't quite known what to strike. Some states, New Mexico, Georgia, were almost untouched, while others—Florida and Texas—had been blasted to bits. Parts of Florida were gone. Where Orlando and Tampa once stood was now a great, jagged, hydrogen bomb-created canal that stretched hundreds of miles across the interior, filled with a red, muddy water.

Slowly life tries to force its way back onto the surface of the ripped and ravaged land. Many forests have expanded over the last century in areas that weren't hit. Great parts of the United States are now thick with brush and trees and resemble the country the way it looked in the 1800s. In other places the deserts cover the earth for four, five hundred miles in every direction — unrelenting, broiling, hot, snake-filled and cactus-dotted obstacles that stand between other living parts of the country.

THE HIDDEN FREE CITIES: Over seventy-five Free American hidden towns have sprung up over the last hundred years. Located at the edges of hot zones, which the Russian troops are reluctant to enter, these towns, hidden in caves, mountains, deep wooded valleys, are made up of armed resistance fighters. Each Free City consists of anywhere from one thousand to forty thousand people. They are fiercely democratic, using town meetings to discuss and vote on all issues.

The Free Americans, who have been bred out in the country, away from the Russian-dominated "clean" areas, have, through natural selection, become ten times more resistant to radiation than their ancestors. They are bred tough, with weak children placed out in the twenty-below zero nights. If the child lives, it is allowed to develop. If not, then it is just as well to put it out of its misery now.

Ted Rockson fights out of Century City — one of the more advanced Free Cities and

10

the manufacturer of the Liberator automatic rifle, used by freefighters everywhere. They attack Russian convoys, blow up bridges. But they plan for the day when they can begin their all-out assault on the enslavers.

THE RUSSIANS: The United Socialists States of America is run by the red-faced, heavy-drinking General Zhabnov, headquartered in the White House, Washington, D.C., now called New Lenin. A bureaucrat, careful but not cunning, and a libertine, Zhabnov spends days eating and nights in bed with young American girls rounded up by his men. Zhabnov has been appointed supreme president of the U.S. for a ten-year period, largely because he is the nephew of the Russian premier Vassily. General Zhabnov rules America as his personal fiefdom. The only rules he must obey—first, no uprisings, and second, seventy-five percent of the country's crops grown by the enslaved American workers must be sent to Russia. General Zhabnov believed once that the situation was good. Now Zhabnov realizes he faces an awesome enemy, Ted Rockson, on the American side, and a power struggle with Killov.

Colonel Killov is the head of the KGB in the U.S., headquartered in Denver, Colorado. He is a ruthlessly ambitious man whose goal it is to someday be premier of the world. Thin, almost gauntly skeletal looking, with a long face, sunken cheekbones and thin lips that spit words, Killov's operatives are everywhere in the country — in the fortresses and the Russian officer ranks, and, lately, he has even managed to infiltrate an American-born agent into the highest levels of the American resistance. Colonel Killov believes General Zhabnov to be a fool. Killov knows that the American forces are growing stronger daily and forming a nationwide alliance to fight together. The calm days of the last century are about to end.

From Moscow, Premier Vassily rules the world. Never has one man ruled so much territory. From the bottom of Africa to Siberia, from Paraguay to Canada, Russian armies are everywhere. A constant flow of supplies and medical goods is needed to keep the vast occupying armies alive. Russia herself did not do badly in the war. Only twenty-four American missiles reached the Soviet Union, and ten of these were pushed off course or exploded by ground-to-air missiles. The rest of the U.S. strike was knocked out of the skies by Russian killer satellites that shot down beams of pure energy and picked them off like clay pigeons.

Vassily is besieged on all sides by problems. His great empire is threatening to break up.

Everywhere there are rebel attacks on Russian troops. In Europe, in Africa, in India, especially in America. The forces of the resistance troops are growing larger and more sophisticated in their operations. Vassily is a highly intelligent and well-read man. He has devoured history books on other great leaders and the problems they faced. "Great men have problems that no one but another great man could understand," he lectures his underlings. Advisers tell him to send in more forces and quickly crush the insurgents. But Vassily believes that to be a tremendous waste of manpower. If it goes on like this he may use neutron bombs again. Not a big strike, but perhaps in a single night, yes, in one hour, they could target the fifty main trouble spots in the world and . . . order must be maintained. For Vassily knows his history. One thing that has been true since the dawn of time — wherever there had been a great empire, there had come a time when it began to crumble.

Chapter One

Something shifted. Deep within the earth, a rumbling and grinding of massive grids of rock hundreds of miles long, pushed against one another, cracking. Something bubbled and boiled like a thing alive. It was the poison of a hundred years, the black rotting radioactive liquids that had seeped into the soil through a million cracks and collected hundreds of miles down in a dark sea of death. It was an underground ocean of stench and decay and rot, of glowing molecules with names like strontium 90, titanium 140 and krypton 85 — all of them as virulent as the day they had been created red hot from the fires of the H-Bombs going off everywhere like the fourth of July a century before. It was a sea of slime and putrescence that writhed in a radioactive frenzy spitting forth clouds of toxic gas, reaching out with pseudopods, of the purest blackness.

The earth around the living lake of death shook

and trembled violently, moving and quivering on every side of the dark sea. It was as if the earth could no longer stand the radioactivity; as if trying to free itself of the poisons, the earth opened up a funnel to the surface of the planet, cracking a thousand-foot-long chasm through its rocky skin. The sea of slime shot toward the surface as if propelled like lava from an erupting volcano as the crack in the earth opened nearly a mile wide, ripping the cactus-dotted prairie like a piece of paper. Black liquid swept out over the parched wastelands by the millions of gallons, the waves of darkness piled high atop one another roaring off in every direction.

The Black Sea shot across the countryside, engulfing, killing every living thing it found. They sank beneath its thirty-foot high wall of noxious slime, instantly drowning or burned to a blistery death by the super high rads contained within. The Ocean of Death swept up everything in its path: Groves of trees disappeared, snapped away like twigs, groundhogs, lizards, rainbirds, giant-horned buffalo all tore for their lives as they heard and saw the poisonous tidal wave approaching. Soon the prairie was alive with a flood of animals that ran just ahead of the River of Darkness. Running as fast as their padded, clawed, or hooved feet could carry them. Each of them knew somewhere in its primitive brain that death was just behind them. That a misstep or fall would mean the end. A wave of life fleeing a wave of death.

Chapter Two

The fangs of the sabre-toothed mountain lion sparkled like chromium ice picks, glistening with saliva in the rays of the setting pink sun. The creature's eyes, narrow and red as blood, were fixed straight ahead on the human who stood in its way. The meanest-looking mountain cat Ted Rockson had ever seen: black spots the size of silver dollars and claws like meathooks came slinking toward him, growling a deep guttural sound that caught in the cat's throat, as if afraid to go past the foot-long curved ivory teeth on each side of its opened jaw.

"Easy boy," Rockson said, stepping slowly backward and to the side. He sensed that the creature was not after him but just wanted to get by. Behind Rock, Charles Langford, his daughter Kim, and Mountain Man Ed, all six feet eight inches of him, stood frozen, their hearts slamming in their chests. The golden-haired mountain lion edged forward. Rockson let his arm drop slowly down to his holster as he placed his thick-veined, sun-darkened hand around the reassuring butt of his .12 gauge shotgun pistol. But he wouldn't kill the thing unless he had to. The sabre-toothed lion, Maximus Felinus, as named by Dr. Schecter's science crew back in Century City, was one of a true new species, created from the omnipresent x-rays, gamma rays, and beta rays, eternal by-products of the H-bombs that had fallen onto America by the thousands. Mutated chromosomes, genetic patterns twisted and rearranged into new forms of life—like the cute killer pussycat that stood in front of them.

The mountain cat took a final wary look at Rockson and his crew, growled loudly, opening its jaws to their nearly two-and-a-half-foot extension, then just as quickly tore past them into the low bushland ahead. Rock let his grip on the shotpistol relax. The others breathed a sigh of relief as he turned.

"Rock, what is it about you?" Kim asked, teasing him. "Wherever you go—cats, hogs, rats, something seems to want to attack you."

"I've got what they call a magnetic personality." Rock smiled back, his violet and aquamarine eyes dancing with energy. "Everything just loves me." Kim looked over at his broad muscled physique, and a chill coursed through her body as she remembered their nights together in the Glower's village just days before.

Mountain Ed, his buckskin jacket flapping, his

three immense antiquated hunting rifles slung over his shoulder, slapping against his back, walked several yards ahead and poked at a bloody animal carcass lying next to some thickly thorned bushes. He carefully avoided the three-inch-long blue barbs of the vegetation just waiting for something to brush against it so it could inject itself and its poison into their flesh.

"That kitty left his dinner, Rock," Mt. Ed snorted, pointing down at a partially consumed young male elk. Rock came over and looked. Only the skull had been cracked open, snapped to pieces inside the powerful jaws of the killer cat. Brain still oozed from one side of the head, cracked like a coconut.

"They go for the brain first," Mt. Ed said, his wiry black beard falling below the thick sun-puffed lips. "Then the heart, kidneys. This one hasn't even touched its skull stew."

"Strange," Rock said, stepping back from the corpse and looking in the direction the cat had come. "They usually don't back down from a challenge. But that one seemed scared. Of what?" If there was something that could scare *that*, Rockson wanted to know what it was and quick.

They both turned suddenly, reaching for their guns as they heard a scrambling in some dense brush just yards away. Three gray wart hogs, their long tusks standing straight as an officer's sword, came rushing toward them. Rock ripped out his pistol, but the usually fierce warted pigs swerved to the right and tore right past the Doomsday Warrior without so much as a glance.

"What the hell's going on?" Charles Langford, the newly elected president of the Re-United States of America grumbled.

"Beats me," Rock said. "But I think maybe we should join them and start heading in that direction." He started down what seemed like some sort of path the animals were following, a slightly trampled-down stretch of bushland about ten feet wide. But it was turning into a superhighway Rockson thought, as a whole new group of animals came flying through the thickets and past them, out onto more open terrain. Not one paid the slightest attention to Rockson or the others, their heads down, their legs pumping like locomotives as they shot by.

Rock kneeled down and put his ear to the earth. He heard something, something he didn't like at all. He had heard the sound once before and he had nearly died.

"Okay folks, I don't want to alarm you," Rock said, looking grimly at Kim. "But we've got to drop everything and run. There's some sort of flood, tidal wave heading this way." They started a medium jog in the direction the animals were heading. Rockson could have run twice as fast but held back with Kim and President Langford who were still recovering from the radiation burns they had received just a month before. The Glower's incredible telepathic healing powers (SEE BOOK #3) along with Rockson's own PSI abilities had cured the two of them, pulling poisoning radiation from their bodies. But still human beings are made of flesh and blood—they had been in deep shock,

20

and Rock wondered how much they could take.

The Doomsday Warrior pulled out a pair of dirty field glasses, a beat-up pair that Mt. Ed had given him, after saving Rock from the same N-bomb blast that had nearly killed Kim and the president.

Now he could see it: a wall of sheerest black, like the side of a mountain, coming straight toward them. And it didn't look like water; Rock could see that from twelve miles away. It was thick and oily and seemed to almost reach forward with pseudopods of its foul grease, grabbing and digesting the poor creatures that hadn't been quick enough. Rock spun the glasses around in the other direction, searching for a rise, a mountain, anything that would get them out of the oncoming deluge.

The sound of the thing came to them: a dull roar, far off, with the power of ten million tons of water, crashing forward, growing with every minute as the black foulness continued to pour from the bowel's of the earth miles away.

There! To the east, perhaps two miles away. Some kind of small hill, Rock could see through the dusty glasses. "This way," he screamed out to the others as more animals continued to rush past them, an old mangy wolf actually brushing against Mt. Ed's leg for a second, too scared to stop and take a bite.

"We've got to go faster," Rock shouted to the president and Kim as they began to falter.

"Can't Rock," the president gasped. "I'm usually much stronger than this but—" He looked humiliated, angry at having to slow down the party. "Rock, leave me," he gasped, lurching around on unsteady legs. "Take Kim and—"

"Don't be ridiculous, Father," Kim said loudly as the four of them stopped as Langford collapsed to the ground, his chest heaving.

"Kim, can you run?" Rock asked the petite blonde, the woman he loved.

"Yes—I—think so, but my fath—"

"Don't worry." Rockson placed both arms under the gasping middle-aged leader of America and swung him up over his right shoulder like a sack of potatoes. The president gasped for a moment and then relaxed, resigned. The three of them began running again, faster than before. Kim's mouth was wide open, sucking in air, and even Mt. Ed, who Rockson knew was made of iron, began to look a little weary. But then he did have over three hundred pounds of flesh on him to carry, not to mention his huge sack of supplies and trio of blunderbusses hung over his shoulders. They tore across the increasingly sparse bushland, just black cactuses and tumbleweeds occupying the yellowish ground.

At last they reached it. Rock laid the president gently at the base of the seventy-five-foot-high hill. Kim and Mt. Ed fell against the soft curve of dirt at the base as Rockson swung the field glasses back behind them. It was there! Larger than ever. With the binoculars it took up nearly the whole lens: a wall of oily water, of some kind of liquid anyway, dark as a moonless night, stretching like a curtain of death across the horizon. What it was, where it came from, Rock would probably never know. Just one of a thousand ways of dying in America 2089 A.D. He gave them thirty seconds to rest and then said firmly, "Let's climb." They protested but rose. The wall of darkness could be seen now with the naked eye as it grew and grew, roaring across the prairie, now less than five miles off. The dull roar was growing to an unnerving rumble that seemed to shake the very ground beneath them.

It wasn't an easy climb, Rock could see that right away. The hill was high enough as the flood didn't look like it would rise over fifty feet, but the sandy, graveled surface of the hill proved difficult to support a strong foothold. Somehow they struggled up the side, kicking dirt in one another's faces, moving up ten feet, sliding down five. Rockson, dragging Langford by one arm, was the first over the top—and he didn't like what he saw. Just thirty feet away near the center of the fifty-foot-wide plateau at the top of the hill stood—stood—Rockson really didn't know what to call it. But he knew he didn't like it—and it didn't like him. He quickly pulled the president up over the side of the embankment as he yelled down to Mt. Ed.

"There's something here; get some of your mini-cannons loaded up. We're going to need them." Rock turned back to face the lizard-thing, now up on its hind legs standing nearly nine feet in the air. It looked vaguely like a snarlizard, a none too pretty development in the gila monster family. But this thing was a monster far beyond any snar Rock had ever seen. Its face was a twisted mess of throbbing green arteries; its jaws, shaped somewhere between an alligator's and a tyrannosaurus rex's snapped at the air, as its long clawed hands opened and closed as if imagining ripping Rockson to pieces. Its entire scaly body, muscles rippling in thighs as thick as Rock's chest, was iridescent green with streaks of barely visible red veins occasionally shining through. But it was the rows of serrated teeth that seemed to take up most of its face—teeth a good eight inches long and curved inward, set on jaws that looked as if they could snap a tree in half.

Rock stood in front of the president who lay moaning on the yellowish crest. He moved slowly to the left, wanting to draw the creature's attention away from Langford. He glanced back as Mt. Ed's hand came looking for a hold over the loose-packed top.

"Careful man," Rockson yelled down. "Move slowly. I don't want to spook this thing." He looked down quickly at the shotpistol, fully loaded. It would take more than a few shots to get that thing. Its scales looked like hammered pieces of half-inch metal, and close to impenetrable. The lizard creature flicked out a long red-forked tongue every few seconds, tasting the air around it. Its orange eyes burned like mini-suns set far back in the huge green head. There was still blood around the creature's black, quarter-sized nostrils. It had eaten only hours before, but now that it realized it was relatively safe from the impending disaster, it felt hungry again. The dim thought of food slowly penetrated the monster's brain and then its musculature. It suddenly dropped into a half crouch, pulling its long snakelike neck down. Its legs bent like springs, ready to pounce. Rock didn't like the posturings at all—the thing was going to strike.

The Doomsday Warrior scanned it quickly up and down for any weakness. Its throat just beneath the lower and larger jaw looked unprotected by scales. It had to be flexible so the lizard could chew and swallow huge chunks of meat. Rock fixed the throat in his mind.

Mt. Ed pulled himself completely up over the side, grabbing the biggest of his rifles as he rolled over onto his stomach.

"Fire!" Rockson yelled from thirty feet down the small plateau. "Distract it." Mt. Ed didn't flinch as he sighted up the ugly predator, aiming for the top of the thigh. Maybe he could sever some muscles, take away its mobility. He pulled the trigger and the six-foot-long crude-looking homemade rifle exploded out a fist-sized shell. The shot dug in just an inch below the spot the mountain man had picked and slammed into one of the lizard's steel-hard scales. The slug bounced off, dropping back onto the soft dirt, though the creature let out a roar of pain and anger. It hissed loudly and leaped toward Mt. Ed, its tongue snapping out, its front arms reaching for the human who was nearly as big as they were. Rockson jumped, too, perpendicular to the creature. Their arcs carried them just past one another, and as Rockson approached he aimed the shotgun pistol at the lizard-thing's throat. Before he could pull the trigger something whipped around his leg and slammed him out of the air to the ground. The creature's seven-foot-long tail — it had caught his foot as it jumped. The thing was amazingly agile. Rock fell to the dirt, the tail letting go instantly as soon as it had knocked him off balance. He hit hard, almost flat on his face and stomach so swift had been the pull of the long green appendage. He shook his head a few times to clear his brain and then rolled over quickly in case the thing was about to land on his back.

But it was engaged in other business. On top of Mt. Ed. The two of them were battling away — a war of the gargantuas. The mountain man was trying to wrestle it to the ground, but it was too strong even for him. It snapped its tail forward and wrapped the end around both of the human prey's legs and pulled. The big fellow who had saved Rockson's life was slammed to the yellow dirt with a loud thwack. He reached for his long hunting blade and had it halfway out when the lizard came in for the kill. Like a snake striking, its head and jaws moved in a blur. It snapped the fearsome rows of teeth into the man's neck and slammed shut with all its strength. Mt. Ed's body shuddered violently as the head was nearly severed from the neck. Blood gushed like a river from the opened gash and splattered out in all directions, onto the lizard and the cold hilltop ground. The thing snapped its tongue in and out of the red neck, sipping the hot blood, slurping it back into the drooling green mouth.

"Oh my God," Rock whispered from about thirty feet. It had all happened so quickly — in seconds, before he had had a chance to react. "You bastard, you slimy ugly bastard," Rockson madly screamed at the thing. He walked forward, aiming the shotpistol.

The lizard-thing looked up, its orange eyes swinging around menacingly, taking in the approach of the human with the fiery pupils of hell itself. Another! Another meal! In its dim mind it wondered why these prey died so willingly. Hardly a fight. It took one last sip of the delicious blood from the cooling corpse, Mt. Ed's buckskin jacket drenched with the sticky redness of his disappearing life. The green scaled mutation jumped up into the air, spinning around in mid-flight, and landed on its long heavily armored legs. It roared out a shriek of contempt and headed toward Rockson, moving with loud slaps of its immense clawed feet. The Doomsday Warrior waited until it was just ten feet away. He knew it was about to leap—he had figured out its style. As it tensed its legs he jumped to the side. The lizard launched itself forward and Rock began firing. He pulled the trigger down once and kept his finger on it. The automatic firing sequence took over, sending a shell down the chamber every third of a second. Rock kept the pistol pointed straight ahead, not letting it bounce back even an inch. The thing had to die! The first shell caught it in the chest and knocked two of its thick scales off. The second shell hit the same spot—minus the green armor plating—and dug deep into the lizard's chest. Green blood began spouting from the holes. The third shot hit it in the stomach and then the groin. The thick hide, only lightly armored down here, was pierced with tiny holes, and the thick green blood began oozing out of the still airborne predator.

It was almost upon him now, wriggling its body in mid-flight as it saw that Rockson had moved off to the side. In spite of its wound it still was strong and alert. Rock could see that: Its eyes glowed with murderous intensity, searching for his flesh. But the Doomsday Warrior stood his ground. He raised the .12 gauge death dealer back up the green body as the hideous face came closer and closer. This time the throat—he let the pistol rip out another three streams of lead death. Two of the x-shaped shot patterns caught the thing just below its jaw where the scales of the upper chest and the scales of its jaws met—here there was only thick leathery hide. The shells tore through the outer layer of lizard flesh and into the thing's throat and windpipe. The entire side of its neck exploded out in a sputum of green and black liquid, tendrils and veins. Yet it continued forward, more dead than alive but determined to take its killer with it. Rock stared into its mad eyes as it fell atop him, firing the final shot directly into the center of the hideous face from just inches away.

The green lizard-thing was on top of him now. Rock tried to roll away, but its immense weight pinned him down. He reached for his knife and grabbed it, swinging it in a swift arc and pumping it into the thing's side again and again. He must have stabbed it fifteen times into a vulnerable spot where some of the armor plating had been ripped away before he realized the thing was dead. If it wanted him it would have had him by now. Rockson pushed up with all his strength. Resting his elbows on the bloody ground and heaving at the same time, he slid out from under it. It was dead all right! Everything above its chest was just a mess of slimy green twisted tissue. His last three shots had butchered the thing. The heart was seemingly unstoppable as it pumped out pulse after pulse of oily seaweed green blood through the nearly foot-wide opening in its neck.

Rockson turned toward the other side of the plateau, not wanting to see what he knew he would see. Mt. Ed was gone. Rock walked slowly over, the empty shotgun pistol dangling like a paralyzed limb at his side. He stood over the American who had saved his life.

"Shit, goddamned shit," the Doomsday Warrior whispered down to the dead man. Whispered to the world, to God, knowing nothing would hear. "You didn't deserve to go this way." The Doomsday Warrior spat out from between clenched teeth. His brilliant eyes sparkled with rage.

Rock suddenly heard a deep groan from his right. The president. Langford was trying to sit up, his hand over his forehead where he had been cut when Rockson had yanked him up over the side. A hand suddenly came over the edge of the hill and a high voice yelled out for help.

"Someone—I can't make it alone." Rock rushed over to Kim and reached down, pulling the small blond daughter of the president of the U.S. up over the edge.

"What happened?" she asked breathlessly. "I

29

heard all that shooting. Is my—" She glanced frantically around until her eyes saw the now sitting Langford. "Thank God," she half cried, rushing toward him, throwing herself around him. "Oh Father, I thought—"

"No, I'm all right, but—" He looked quickly to the other side of the rise and then back again. Kim turned her eyes and saw the bloody red thing, the head totally ripped from its body, that had once been the mountain man.

"Oh no—" She burst into tears and jumped up into Rockson's arms. "I can't be, it can't be," she muttered over and over again.

"Shh, it's all right," Rock said, cradling her sweet-smelling body that contrasted so bizarrely with the fetid stench of the bloody charnel ground that the hilltop had been turned into.

"He's gone now. No more pain," the Doomsday Warrior said, holding the woman he loved with all his might.

Chapter Three

The flood of foulest blackness grew closer as screaming animals continued to hurtle by below flying like arrows shot from a bow, running as they had never run before. Some tried to get up the hill where Rock, Kim, and the president were, but most plummeted back down, their scampering claws or hooves too frantic to get the footholds necessary for the ascent. A few creatures made it to the top but Rockson didn't fire, letting them take up shelter at the other end of the plateau where they eyed the humans and each other nervously — three desert goats, a smallish mountain panther, and some kind of unicorned species of mountain elk that Rock had never seen before, two of them, with a long straight horn coming from the center of their white heads, extending nearly six feet up. The creatures snorted and looked anxiously around, but all the animals seemed content to make a momentary truce with one another in view of the common danger.

The front waves of the black wall slammed into the lower portion of the hill sanctuary. They could actually feel the thud and shaking of the entire dirt structure as the dark waters pressed from all sides. The crest of the dark flood was filled with debris and struggling animals screaming out bloody murder as they floated past. It was a horrible sound, the barks and growls and roars of hundreds of prairie creatures who hadn't moved fast enough. They quickly sank into the black stickiness and an even more ghastly silence descended around the hill. After the initial waves the flood seemed quite calm, except that it kept rising. At first it was only about thirty feet above the prairie floor, but gradually the black sea seemed to move up a foot every minute or so. Rockson kept a careful eye on the rising waters, although what they would do if it came over the top he had no idea. There was nowhere else to go.

They heard a loud commotion as a huge felled tree came by with a whole passenger list of raccoons screaming out their fear and indignation at having their home so rudely dragged up by its roots and buffeted downstream. But they hung on tenaciously with enough presence of mind to gobble down each waterlogged bug that stumbled drunkenly from the innards of the nearly eighty-foot-long, six-foot-thick tree. The sun had long since set, but the stars shone down like rows of beacons, giving the night air and the flood an eerie translucent quality, everything shining and bob-bing.

When the sea of death passed the sixty-foot mark, Rockson heard the lapping suddenly increase and rushed to the edge of the hill. The black sea seemed to be rushing faster now as if spurred on from behind. There wasn't a hell of a lot more breathing room and Rockson could see through the darkness that the river was glowing just beneath the surface. He didn't have his wrist geiger with him — it had been ripped from him in the neutron blast — but he had seen enough of the atomic death in his life to know — it was high rad. Super high rad. If they fell in the stuff they would die. Cooked like lobster in an atomic pot. The three of them sat at the edge of the hill looking down as the sickly black tide rose higher and higher. Nothing that had fallen in its grasp lived. The bloated carcasses of animals were already floating to the surface, their eyes filled with oily mud, their bodies oozing with every radioactive poison known to man, their hides glowing from the megadoses of the atomic liquid.

Kim sat next to Rockson and put her arms around him. At least if she was going to die it would be with the man she loved. The flood slowed but continued to rise, relentlessly, inexorably as if its sole mission on earth now was to get *them*. Through the long night it moved, flowing more slowly as miles behind, the earth at last ceased its violent vomit of the underground sea of poison. The chasm closed up and the last of the black liquid surged forward. Slowly the sea of death dropped down, sinking once again into the loose soil, but this time dispersed over twenty-five hundred square miles, its power, its radioactivity broken down into less virulent levels.

As the pumpkin orange sun rose from out of the purple steam of night, it seemed to push back the waters. The morning sky was laced with a spiderweb of strontium green webs as clouds of radioactive dust circled high above the earth.

At last the waters sank, dropping back through a million burrows and cracks. Soon they were gone, leaving a slimy deposit of black tar on the prairie floor. The animals who had cowered on the plateau saw it was time to leave, and each did so, taking off in different directions, scampering down the hillside and onto the plains. The ground was smoking slightly and it burned thier feet, but they would survive. They ran howling and baying at the brightly burning morning sun, happy just to be alive.

Rock got them organized or as organized as he could with a sick older man and and frightened woman. Kim had been really shaken by Mt. Ed's death. Rock was, too. But he didn't show things like that. There would be time for vulnerability later. Not now when death was on every side. He walked over to the dead mountain man and began a prayer that the freefighters said over the fallen bodies of their comrades—if there was time—if the Reds weren't hot on their trail with their screaming MIGs and Blackshirt choppers. He looked down at the bloody corpse, his head bowed as Langford and Kim stood silently behind him.

"Take this man, God, into your heaven
Whatever and wherever it may be
And know that this man, Mountain Ed, was a

good and brave American
Who gave everything that he had
So that others might live. Amen."

Rockson coughed gruffly, stuffing more shells into his pistol. Kim and her father shuffled awkwardly behind him.

"Okay folks, we're going to get going. I know both of you aren't feeling too hot — but — I don't like this whole area here. There's something about it. I sense that the land is poisoned beyond the norm."

"You mean we don't have time for a picnic," Kim said trying to break the tension.

"If we stay here we'll *be* the picnic," Rock cracked back. They loaded up their remaining supplies, Rockson taking Mt. Ed's backpack, and headed back down the hill onto the slightly soggy ground. The ground was hot as the boiling temperature of the waters slowly cooled. They walked forward onto a wasteland that seemed to have no end. Everywhere were the remains of death. All that the black flood had swept up and destroyed it had deposited again onto the caked prairie ground. Animals everywhere — their slime-coated bodies in frozen sculptures of death, some with their jaws still snarling, trying to fight off death to the end. Others were twisted into a fetal position, trying to pretend as the end came that it was all just a dream, an animal's dark nightmare. They lay bloated, thick as waterlogged wood as flies began gathering around the rancid corpses.

Behind them the body of Mt. Ed shifted weirdly, the stomach moving in little waves. The eggs of the lizard-thing—nearly twenty of them that the creature had deposited into the human's stomach with a flick of its long tail, a tail that doubled as its sex organ, moved inside the corpse, twisting and eating. Eating everything in their path, and when they had consumed their host whole from the inside out, they would hatch, little green lizard-things, a foot long, into a world of unfathomable danger.

On the surface of the corpse ants began crawling. First just a few, then hordes. Marching in long lines, the eaters of the dead converged, searching for the wounded, the rotting. They covered the cold mountain man with a blanket of moving blackness, a million little mandibles taking their piece of the pie.

Chapter Four

Flies were everywhere. Rock, Kim, and the president had to continually swat at their faces and hands. The creatures were in a state of frenzy at so much death to dine on spread out across the corpse-strewn prairie. The buzzing insects seemed unable to tell the difference between the living and the dead as they dove in kamikaze squadrons against the freefighters' flesh.

"Damn, these fucking flies—they're driving me mad," Langford barked out suddenly. Rock stopped and looked. The president's face was already swelling up from the countless little nips. The Doomsday Warrior took off Mt. Ed's pack and pulled out one of two gourds of water stored within. Out here in the middle of nowhere water was more precious than gold, but Langford was obviously in trouble. Rock wetted down a flannel shirt from the pack and handed it to Langford who covered his head and shoulders. It worked. The flies buzzed angrily around the protective shielding and then tore off, too confused to waste more time. Rockson made two more instant shields for Kim and himself.

After three hours of marching through a virtual graveyard of rotting corpses, they came to the now nearly closed chasm through which the black bile had emerged. It was now only about six feet wide at its narrowest point. Rock could see instantly that they'd have to jump it or detour for miles around the jagged ripped earth that stretched off in each direction as far as the eye could see. He jumped first, throwing the backpack across and then taking a running start. He cleared the seemingly bottomless crack with ease and turned to help the others if they had trouble. Kim came next, flying gracefully over the divide and landing on both feet. Then it was Langford's turn. He took a long lumbering stride and jumped. He cleared the chasm but his foot just caught the other side which crumbled out from under him. Rockson reached forward and grabbed the president just as he was sliding backward into eternity. He yanked him up and pulled him forward onto terra firma.

"I feel like such an idiot," Langford muttered, looking down. "Everything I do seems to self-destruct." The president was used to being a strong and vigorous man. He had spent half his life traveling around to the hidden cities of America, spreading the idea of a new United States, a president, and a government. A reborn America that would unite and throw the Reds out once and for all. His years in the wastelands, trekking across the heartland of the country, had made him tough, resourceful. But then — at the very moment of his greatest triumph — his election by the ReConstitutional Convention to the office of president, the Russians with a spy planted in the freefighters' midst had dropped two neutron bombs, wiping out nearly ninety percent of the delegates from every Free City in America. Langford was deeply depressed about the decimation of the newly formed government. It had lasted all of an hour before the mushroom clouds had fried flesh into crumbling charcoal. The shortest reign in history, Langford thought bitterly to himself. And his body didn't feel too hot either. Ever after the Glowers had worked their magic on himself and Kim, his legs were wobbly, his gums blistered and sore, his stomach constantly churning as if about to vomit. The human body could only take so much. He was falling into a deep depression made only worse by the realization that he, of all people, was the elected moral and spiritual leader of the free men and women of America — and he had nothing more to give.

"Please sir, don't talk about yourself that way," Rock said, looking nervously down at the ground. "You don't have to apologize to me. As the commander-in-chief of the new United States, I and every other freefighter are at your command."

"I'll let you do the commanding, Rock," Langford said with the first grin he had shown for days. "If you don't mind, I'd probably guide us into quicksand or something."

They headed on for hours. Rock carefully gauged the skin tone and breathing of his two charges. Both were putting everything they had into the endless walking. Rock remembered when Kim and he had first met, naked in a Russian jail cell.* How she had offered her untouched body to him that night — before the KGB swine could get their hands on her the next morning. She was tough. In her own way as tough as Rockson.

After nearly a day of stumbling across the parched land on the other side of the chasm they reached higher ground where there began to be a little more life: wildly colored flowers, shrubs that rose nearly twenty feet into the air. They had gone from an almost dead zone to fertile terrain in just over fifteen miles. The three of them looked around in amazement as the lushness of the land grew in leaps and bounds. Here, fruits — pink and red and green — hung down tantalizingly from vines and trees, fields of rainbow flowers, petals as large as dinner plates, blazing with a glory all their own, slowly closing as the ochre sun beat down from the late afternoon western sky.

"Can we — " Kim asked, reaching up and plucking a greenish pink banana-shaped fruit from a stalk.

"Yeah, these are all right," Rock answered, grabbing a few himself. "I remember eating some like these a few years ago. Didn't die — but they were sour." They peeled back the thick moist skins and took tentative bites.

"These are sweet as sugar," Kim said, taking bite after delicious bite. The three of them gorged themselves, having not eaten for nearly two days. The fresh fruit and leafy rich vegetables they found growing wild everywhere made them feel much more positive. Even Langford's face seemed to relax and glow with color. Not everything was wasteland. It was as if

*See Doomsday Warrior #2

nature was giving them a reprieve—a moment's rest and nourishment before the realities of a harsh world would again bare its fangs.

"Must have been farms here once," Rockson said as they walked slowly on through fields of edible produce now bizarrely twisted and colored from the low rad radioactive soil. "See how things are growing in their own geometric areas—mostly squares." He pointed out the nearly straight-lined fields. "All pink fruits there and these green leafy plants here—looks like—lettuce I think they used to call it. This must have once been a big farm belt. Probably didn't take any direct hits—just enough rads to kill off the farmers but not the farms."

"Enough radiation to produce some pretty strange breeds," Kim said, picking up a tomato nearly as large as a grapefruit. She cut it open—just like the real thing—seeds spat out as big as grapes. "Now, if we just had some spaghetti." She smiled. "I'd fix us all a real down-home American meal."

They picked as much of the fruit and vegetables as possible so they'd have fresh supplies. Rockson knew this kind of paradise couldn't go on for very long. But he noted their approximate location on his pocket mapgrid. Back at Century City, agricultural researchers were trying to assemble a nationwide picture of the remaining fertile areas. Someday large-scale agricultural production would begin again. Someday.

They rested for the night under a grove of the fragrant banana trees filled with a small fingerlike fruit that was even sweeter than the others. They fell asleep, Rock with his pistol in his hand, fingers gripped tightly around it. The night sky was unusually clear with nary a trace of the strontium clouds high above. The endless galaxies flickered like lights on a shore signaling the weary traveler's return to peace and safety.

In the middle of the night they were awakened by movement all around them. Rock leaped up, his pistol at the ready. Above him, rustling through the high fruit trees, he could see sets of eyes and little rows of pearly teeth. Suddenly a face darted close—monkeys. Goddamned little golden-skinned monkeys. Rockson had never seen one live but had perused scores of pictures from nature books of the last century. Not to mention the Tarzan movies, among the two thousand films in the Century City archives, shown three times a week, rotating the entire collection. Rock had seen more films of the mid-twentieth century than most people of that time had. He was religious about only one thing—knowledge of the past. After his parents had been killed, tortured, and murdered by a roving band of KGB thugs out for kicks, Rock had made his way armed with just a knife across the vast plains of the American heartlands. When he had reached Century City he had been amazed at the size and scope of the underground complex and had quickly taken advantage of its offerings, spending months in the library and film rooms. Though a constant truant at the C.C. school, his rebellious nature chafing at the bit at having to follow rules and sit in one place all day, Rockson had quickly amassed a great store of information on his own. Knowledge was power. He had known even as a teen that every little fact he could assimilate might someday save his life.

"What are they Rock?" Kim asked nervously, standing closely by his side for safety.

"Monkeys they were called. Came originally from Africa. There must have been some sort of zoo or circus around here once. These things escaped and survived—and seem to be doing quite well. They sure can breed." He looked around—there were hundreds of eyes peering down from above, hidden in the twisting vines of the banana grove. The small, furry, big-eyed primates didn't seem frightened by the human presence nor eager to attack. They leaped from branch to branch, eating their fill of fruit. They chirped wildly to one another in a chorus of monkey gossip beyond the comprehension of the human species.

Somehow the three freefighters fell asleep again, amused by the monkeys and in a strange way, reassured. They dozed more easily as if protected by their chattering childlike relatives and slept soundly through the long night.

They awoke early just as the blazing blood-red sword of the sun arched up into the black and blue flesh of the dying night. They walked for days, the land slowly changing from fertile to a more desolate terrain dotted with thorny shrubs and an occasional jackrabbit. The sky became somewhat overcast which suited Rockson just fine. As long as the big brown and purple cumulus clouds were hanging up there like boulders about to fall, the Reds would have a hard time using their spy drones: those buzzing pilotless cylinders with nothing but stubby wings and video cameras mounted in the nose and stomach of the metal craft to spy down on the world below them.

If the Russians caught them out here in the open . . .

By the fifth day after the black flood, Rock knew they were getting near the location of the president's now bombed-out ranch where the convention had been held. The land grew more rocky; small hills were beginning to turn into the very edge of a mountain range.

"Do you want to go back to the convention site?" Rock asked President Langford as they headed up and down the sloping crabgrassed hills.

"I have to, Rock. Whoever's left there—there must be some who survived—you did—we did. I'll reorganize. There's no other choice. We can't stop this journey of ours. Our trip toward liberation and freedom. There's no turning back—only one way—forward." Langford seemed to be regaining his strength, both physical and mental. His eyes burned once again with the fire of leadership.

"Yes, I know," Rockson answered softly. But he wasn't thinking of Langford, he was thinking of Kim. Being separated from her again—not knowing where she would be or what was happening to her. In many ways he didn't like being in love. It hurt. It created an Achilles' heel in his otherwise almost impenetrable psychic shield. He never had to worry about anyone before. And he never worried for himself. His death was a matter for the gods to decide. He had seen enough to know that when death came knocking, no creature on earth could keep the door closed. The Doomsday Warrior kept his thoughts to himself but turned and looked at her with a feeling of infinite tenderness.

They marched through the lower hills and then up

onto the higher rocky slopes by the second day. Mountain goats sure-footedly jumped around them as eagles and hawks flew slow deliberate circles far above, searching with their razor-sharp eyes for the flash of a cottontail or the rush of a raccoon. The land was again rich and vibrant here and made them relax. They took in the perfumed scents of wood and sap and life itself. Out there on the wastelands it was as if they were on an alien planet with something out to get them. But here—this was their land. Tall trees and green everywhere, wildlife crashing through the thick forests, all in harmonious symbiosis.

They were just coming over a rise above a narrow wooded valley as the sun sank into the cloud-covered pit of night, when Rock held his arm up for them both to be quiet.

"I smell smoke—just ahead. Stay here," he whispered, motioning for them to lie down in the thick, blue-tinged grass. He edged forward cautiously, his shotpistol in his right hand, and rolled quickly over the top of the rise and down a few feet behind a grove of thornbushes.

Voices! He could hear mumbles and the crackling of a fire ahead. And food—the sizzling aroma of fresh-killed venison. It couldn't be Reds. The Russians would never be camping out in the wilds. They preferred a protective circle of tanks and choppers flying overhead. But he had encountered enough bandits, even cannibals, to know that just being Americans didn't guarantee safety from strangers. He slid down the hill at the north side of the two hundred-foot-deep valley, darting from shadow to shadow. It was English all right, he could hear as he

45

drew closer, and laughter.

No—it couldn't be, he thought, disbelieving what his own perceptions were telling him. He moved down the slope and pushed aside the side of a brown, spiked bush. Four men sat around a fire on pieces of a fallen tree. One of them was cooking over low flames, humming softly to himself. *It was*—McCaughlin—and the Rock team. A sardonic smile passed over Rockson's face as he rose and stepped forward, both hands raised.

"All right boys, don't shoot me now," the Doomsday Warrior said, walking toward them. "I'm here to surrender." They looked up, startled at the sound of the voice. Then their eyes lit up like Christmas bulbs on the trees of their ruddy faces.

"Holy shit, as I live and breathe," Detroit Green's ebony dark face broke out in a wide grin. The bull-like man said, "He done returned from the dead." He spoke in a mocking southern accent, almost dropping the piece of venison he held in his hand. They just sat there looking up, their jaws hanging open as if struck dumb. McCaughlin, Archer, even Chen couldn't make a sound.

"It's me boys, but you look in such a somnabulant state right now that if I make a speech I'm afraid you might pass out." They jumped up and rushed over to their leader, the man they were sure had been killed. The team gathered around him, slapping the Doomsday Warrior on the back, wanting to make body contact with Rockson, to make sure it wasn't just a pipe dream, to touch the flesh of his breathing body.

"How the fuck did you—"Detroit began, tilting his ebony face sideways above the broad sweatshirt-covered chest.

"It's a long story," Rock said. "Too long. And you? I was sure you all were a group of charcoal statues I found."

"We saw 'em, too," Chen piped in, running his hand along the dark mustache that curved down across his Oriental mouth, below the deep almond eyes. "In fact when we scoured these hills we found scores of them." The Chinese martial arts master was nearly invisible in his neck-to-toe black ninja suit. Only the flames of the fire flickering over his face showed the presence of a man.

Rock turned to Archer. The huge near-mute was smiling with a grin as broad as his watermelon-sized face. He cradled his immense steel crossbow in one arm and squeezed Rockson around the shoulder with the other, almost lifting him off the ground. At seven feet plus and at least four hundred pounds, although no one had ever really been able to weigh him, the man had the strength of a grizzly bear.

"He likes you, Rock." Detroit laughed. "He was sure looking blue in the face when we all thought you wasn't around no more. We were thinking of electing a new team leader, but we all just looked at each other and said—no way."

"Wasn't the same without you, Rock," McCaughlin piped in back at the fire where he was tending his venison à la campfire. "Kinda' like steaks without no steak sauce."

"I'm touched," Rockson said, putting his hand with the shotgun pistol across his chest.

"Well, if we waited for a signal from you to tell us things were all right," a woman's voice suddenly said from the edge of the clearing, "we'd be up there all night." Kim and Langford walked over to the fire. The men all saluted with respect. They had been at the ReConstitutional Convention as well and knew who Charles Langford was. They stood at attention, even McCaughlin rising. They were all freefighters and as such, part of the newly formulated United States Army. It sounded good—the U.S. Army.

"Please, please!" Langford said, waving his hands for them all to sit down. "No formalities out here. It seems ridiculous." The president stood on one leg, rubbing the other. Now that they had stopped walking, cramps were beginning to set in.

"Here sir," Chen said, offering his log seat to Langford. "Sit down—we have food ready."

"Good, good." Langford smiled, dropping to the log with a long exhale of relaxation. The moon was starting to rise now casting a ghostly glow over the assembled freefighters. But at least for now they were safe. And there was food. Things could be a lot worse. And would be.

Chapter Five

In Washington, President Zhabnov, supreme commander of the United Socialist States of America—the U.S.S.A.—tossed and turned in his large feather bed trying to wake himself from a nightmare. Two young girls, hardly in their teens, lay on each side of him. One was a twelve-year-old Negress, the other a little blond-haired thing. Both were as smooth and formless as children. But the Russian president of America liked them that way. The girls shifted uncomfortably away from the fat hairy man who slept between them, praying that he wouldn't "take them" again. He had hurt them so.

But Zhabnov had other things on his mind: Killov! Colonel Killov was chasing him, even in his dreams. Was there no escape from the skull-faced madman? Deep in sleep the KGB commander followed him, haunting, threatening. Zhabnov was running down a long well-lit hallway—a hospital corridor, and someone was after him. Then Zhabnov was slipping. He looked down. The shiny white floor was red with blood, a sea of blood coming out from under every door. Then the doors opened and dead men, corpses, their faces pale blue, their arms held out stiffly in front of them, came at him. They opened their lipless jaws to bite at him. Then they were all over the "supreme president," ripping at his flesh. Killov stood behind them, commanding them to kill, to "eat the pig." Zhabnov screamed again and again. Then he awoke.

The obese Red general sat bolt upright in the master bedroom of the White House. The portrait of Franklin Roosevelt stared down through the darkness from across the wide, oak-paneled suite. The wide feather bed was soaked down the middle with his sour sweat. Zhabnov reached over and pushed one of a row of buttons on a control panel mounted on the bedboard, nearly crushing the little three-breasted Negress beneath him. Within seconds the door opened and a servant rushed in, snapping on the wall light.

"A drink man, make me a drink right away! Triple bourbon with ice—quick, quick!" He shook his hand impatiently, then wiped it across his goateed red-flushed face. His hair was thinning on top, just wisps flattened down over the shiny skull, his big stomach and breast-fat chest hung out in the air, shiny with cold sweat. The servant, an ancient pale-faced Ukrainian who trembled as he walked and spoke with aristocratic accent, quickly and expertly poured the drink from Zhabnov's long cherry wood bar that popped out of a paneled wall with the flick of a dial. He brought the bourbon over and handed it to the supreme president, not daring to even glance down at the two naked forms surrounding Zhabnov.

"Go! Go!" Zhabnov waved his hand and the servant rushed out, shutting the lights and gently closing the door behind him.

Zhabnov took a deep gulp from the glass. Three ice cubes just as he liked it, floating, clanking together at the top of the artificially frosted crystal. Within seconds he felt the wonderful glow of alcoholic fire sweep through his gullet, and a warm glow rushed over his face. What the hell was he worried about? He could handle everything. Premier Vassily was allied with him now—against Killov. Even the "Grandfather" had realized Killov's threat, especially after the conspiracy of the doctors, when Killov's physician agents had tried to poison and kill the premier with injections of cancer cells. (See Book #1.)

But the premier had survived and given Zhabnov the word. No more would there be a careful balance of power between the three of them—the Communist trinity that ruled the world. Now it was the premier and Zhabnov to the death against Killov.

"He must be stopped," Vassily had said to Zhabnov over and over on his last call. "The man is mad. He wants to destroy the earth." Zhabnov had never heard the premier so frightened. But now President Zhabnov had his own band of assassins

51

after the colonel of the dread Blackshirted KGB. Killov would never know when or where they would strike — or how they would kill him. One of them would succeed. Of this Zhabnov was sure. He finished the drink and felt much better. He turned toward the small blond girl and put his thick hand on her soft, lithe thigh.

"Come here, little one," the supreme president said, squeezing her young flesh. "Come to me." He grabbed the sub-teen who tried to feign sleep and pulled her atop his aroused, obese body.

In Moscow, Premier Vassily, the "Grandfather," ruler of all the world — from the tip of South Africa to the Siberian Steppes, from Argentina to Canada — sat in his wheelchair on the intricate marble terrace overlooking Red Square. Below him, crowds filed past, petty functionaries heading home from their bureaucratic positions, their long days of stamping and denying requests from around the Soviet Empire. They trudged through the snowy streets several feet deep from the early fall snows as more flakes licked down from the turgid sky, thick with undulating Arctic clouds ready to deposit yet another load of their frozen moisture onto the Red capitol below.

The premier turned to the last page of *The Phemonology of Mind*, by Hegel, the philosopher who had created the ideas from which Karl Marx had written *Das Kapital* and *The Communist Manifesto* among others. The books that had shaken the world. Were still shaking the world. It was hard to believe sometimes the power of words, of writing. Two books had caused such explosive reverberations. From Marx, Lenin, and Trotsky, then Stalin, all the way up to the present — Vassily, an unbroken line of leaders who had carried out *The Communist Manifesto* with a vengeance. Vassily was highly aware of his place in history. He hadn't asked to become ruler of the world. But once he had begun rising in the Red hierarchy, had seen that his intellect and ambitions were of greater power than those around him, the outcome had been inevitable. There are those who are born to rule — must rule. It was beyond the desires of a man. He, Vassily, had been trapped by the forces of history to run things. To run everything. And so he did, and so he would until the day he died.

But there were problems — many. His grip on the world was slipping. Vassily, ever the pragmatist, could see it all clearly. The reports he received via satellite from the far-flung legions, much like Romans, he thought, remembering his history — with their isolated fortresses trying to hold back the barbarian hordes — told him that things were heating up. Every day brought more disquieting reports of rebellion, crop failures, sabotage, attacks on his forces. Years before they had all just been skirmishes, guerilla attacks — a Russian soldier stabbed in the throat in a godforsaken back alley — in Morocco, in Afghanistan, in Brazil. But now the subject peoples were growing more dissatisfied with their lot — and bolder. They had been promised more for years. More food, more autonomy — under the stern gaze of their Red rulers. But nothing had come to pass. The Soviet Empire needed more and more of the raw materials and the few goods that these subjugated countries could produce. The Soviet machine was like some starving creature that ate all that it received and instead of being satisfied just grew hungrier and hungrier. The Soviet peoples in Mother Russia had gotten used to having everything delivered to them. Their own agricultural system had deteriorated to the point where it only supplied about a third of Russia's needs. Everything had to be "imported," a euphemism for taking whatever was needed, and leaving the natives to eke out whatever meager survival they could.

Even the Russian factory system had fallen apart. Little was being produced anymore—other than military equipment and ammunition. The world was slowly falling back into a primitive mode of existence. Industrial technology had been forgotten in the empire over the last century. Each decade the ability to build new machinery, tools, cars, computers, electronic components had fallen farther behind. The Reds had let their high technology at the time of the Great War go fallow, using the vast armaments they had already stockpiled with which to rule. A huge class of "servicers," as they were called, had been able to keep most of the machinery going—constantly oiling the equipment, cleaning the immense factories, replacing worn parts from a dwindling stockpile. But this could only go on for so long.

Only the immense Satellite and ICBM Control Complex on the outskirts of Moscow was kept at peak efficiency—a budget of nearly two billion rubles a year was required just to keep the huge military installation from falling apart. Two fifty-story buildings sat on each side of a steel/magnesium, plastic-coated dome nearly eight hundred feet high that controlled the spy sats, the killer sats, and the guidance system for the armada of remaining Red missiles. The satellites that had shot down the American missiles from the skies as they streamed toward Mother Russia like so many tin ducks in a shooting gallery. Laser beams and particle beams arcing down from the dark heavens like bolts of white-hot lightning, disabling the U.S. weapons so they plummeted into the sea and sank to the depths of the ocean floor.

The giant control center really wasn't needed any longer—as Red intelligence confirmed that no other country on earth had any remaining nuclear weapons. All the nukes were within the Red domain now—an ace in the hole in case the rebels around the world got the upper hand. Not that Premier Vassily wanted to use them. The planet had been poisoned enough already by radioactive pollution. The fertile regions within Russia had been cut to nearly a quarter—and the same was true everywhere. Vast deserts now stood where once fields of crops had danced in the clear sun. But now the sun was sickly and pale as it tried to beat its way through the dust and strontium clouds that continued to circle high above the earth.

Sometimes he felt so tired. Vassily ruled a crumbling empire and deep inside he knew it, though he would never admit it, even to himself. Somehow he had to buy time, to work out accommodations with the rebels so the Russian Empire could at least remain dominant if not in total control. Nearly twenty million Red troops were dispersed around the earth—the largest occupying army in history, and the supplies needed for the bureaucratic backup to support such a force was immense. And things were getting worse, not better. The empire he had taken over in bloody purges in the Kremlin nearly thirty years before was falling apart. Half of southern Asia was no longer in his firm grasp. The war lords there—Asians and rebellious Russian army officers—had created their own little fiefdoms where they ruled with even more of an iron fist than the regular army. China was on fire, under the control of the fanatical *Muabir*, the Flame of Allah. His armies of horse riding, religious zealots were only too willing to die to reach paradise. They attacked huge Russian convoys now, losing thousands of their men in the process, but causing increasing damage as they armed themselves with stolen rifles and even heavy artillery. Indochina was exploding in a renewal of Buddhism, as monks burned themselves and roused their people to rebellion. How could you kill people who killed themselves?

Premier Vassily felt another one of his migraines coming on and pushed the button on the small wireless transmitter affixed to the side of his electric wheelchair. America—that was the worst of all. The freefighters, as they called themselves, were growing bolder by the day—and now they apparently possessed some new secret weapon that had destroyed several Red convoys—if destroyed was the word. He had received reports that nothing but fused metal had been left of nearly a two thousand man, thirty tank force. His scientists couldn't even discover what the technology behind the weapon was. How was it possible that rebels living in caves could produce such miracles of death. Unless? Unless the American fighters were far more advanced than either Killov or Zhabnov realized.

And Killov himself—ready to battle it out with Vassily for control of the world. No longer content to play his role behind the scenes, the KGB commander was directly challenging the Red Army. It was too much—too much. Somehow he had to make a move. If only he could make peace with some of the rebel rulers in each country—buy them off. Or even—he hated the word—make some sort of *concessions*. If he could get the legendary Ted Rockson to join forces with his and Zhabnov's regular army in the U.S.S.A. they could defeat the mad KGB colonel once and for all.

The headache slammed into his skull like howitzer shells. Suddenly a soft cultured voice spoke up just behind him.

"Sir, I have your brandy and some of the pain killers that seemed to help last week." It was Ruwanda Rahallah, Vassily's black African servant whom he had taken to trusting and confiding in more and more these days. Vassily was surrounded on every side by spies and assassins. There were so few men he could trust. But he knew the tall, black ebony African was one of them. Vassily let his grim face relax and he smiled.

"Ah, thank you my friend. You are always here when I need you." Rahallah, once an African prince of the Masai Tribe of East Africa, snatched by Reds when just a child to become a slave back in Russia—now the aide and confidante to the most powerful man in the world, handed the premier two opium pills and then his glass of afternoon brandy. Vassily swallowed the tablets down instantly with a slug of the rich golden brandy. Within seconds he felt the headache diminishing. Rahallah stood still, resplendent in his stiffly creased white tuxedo and white gloves, attentive, awaiting his master's any request. His strong sculpted face with high cheekbones reflected the setting sun's greenish rays as they pierced the twisting storm clouds overhead. He looked almost frightening, like some war mask from times long ago. Vassily shuddered slightly, whether from the cool evening air or the vision of Rahallah's primitive past—he couldn't tell.

"What do you think about?" Vassily asked the African. "Beneath that calm exterior, what goes on in that black mind of yours? I know you're a smart man, probably more intelligent than my entire staff. What? What, tell me!" The premier was agitated. Tonight everything seemed threatening, ominous.

"I think only of how I can serve you, sir," Rahallah said with a stony face. "I've been with you for many years. And I've come to know you for what you are—a good man—trapped by the exigencies of history. You've done well. As well as you can with what you have."

"But don't you ever grow afraid? Angry? Vengeful? After all, your people are still subjects. Work hard—die young. Don't you—" For the first time ever, Vassily suddenly had the terrifying image of Rahallah's strong black hand coming in to kill him in the middle of the night—a knife, a razor.

"Sir, you have promised me that someday my people will be free. My tribe. We have been enslaved by one race or another for centuries. We have learned to be patient, to move with the changing seasons, ride the ever-shifting winds of time. I have been given the opportunity by the gods to come and work for you. Influence you. I speak to you of peace—always. When you ask me for aid in your musings, I whisper peace. In your sleep I whisper peace. Peace for the world—for all mankind—so that we may return to the paradise that this green planet once was. That is my anger, my vengeance—to influence you, sir, to create peace."

Vassily looked very thoughtful for several moments, then glanced up sharply. "Peace—if only it were so easy. I know I've promised you freedom for your tribe. I wish things were calmer. I've been waiting until the empire was firmly in control before I give more power to my subjects. In the midst of revolts is not the time to give in. It is a bad sign. They would be emboldened. I'm sorry, Rahallah—it is not yet time."

"I know you will do what is right," Rahallah answered with a calmness that almost angered Vassily. *He* didn't feel calm. He felt his own anger rising—at always being inundated with requests, favors, crop failures, uprisings. The world was spinning around him like a gyroscope out of control.

"I feel tired tonight, Rahallah. So tired. I'm growing old and there is still much to do. I must leave the planet a safer place. Not more dangerous. But I fear that is what is happening. With this madman Killov making his bid for power. I am the only one who can stop him. My fat fool of a nephew, Zhabnov, is incapable of fighting the cleverness of *The Skull*."

"You are still strong, sir. I know your time has not yet come. I have spoken with the spirits of my ancestors — they have never failed me, never lied to me. Death knocks but cannot break down the wall to your soul. It is my duty to give you what comforts a man, to calm your mind and heart so that you can better deal with the battles of your rule."

"Thank you, Rahallah. Your words always give me comfort. Wheel me in now, I grow cold." The black servant, descended from a warrior race, slowly pushed the wheelchair of the ruler of all the worlds — a frail old man who hardly weighed more than a child. A rotting body, nothing now but skin and veins that seemed they must surely explode out with his life's blood. But the eyes were clear. Clear as the stars that glittered on the stage of the Russian night. And in his mind those eyes were focused on the body of Colonel Killov. Might his death come soon.

The commander of all KGB forces in America stared out from the eightieth floor of the Monolith — the headquarters of the dreaded Blackshirts in the U.S.S.A. Located dead center of what had been Denver, Colorado, the huge black, glass and steel structure was a constant reminder to the American workers for miles around that their pitchforks and axes were nothing compared to the power of the KGB. The Monolith was a monument to death as its two hundred-foot-wide circular frame pierced the morning sky like a dark spear. The veiny red rays of the sun slowly cracked across the vast cobalt blue sky above the Rocky Mountains.

Colonel Killov popped another Benzedril, his twelfth that night. He had been up for nearly four days now and had hardly eaten a bite of food. His sustenance had been reduced to two glasses of vegetable juice pumped with megadoses of vitamins each day. His gaunt skull-like face, cheekbones popping out like bones through rotting flesh, stared back at him from the blue-tinted bullet-proof floor-to-ceiling glass that surrounded his entire eightieth floor suite of offices and living quarters. His flesh had the ghastly color of decayed dough, almost greenish. Killov's eyes were wide open, straining in their sockets like black marbles reflecting the tentative beams of American sunlight that tried to slice into the room.

Killov slammed his thin hand hard against the thick glass and cursed out loud. "Damn that bastard, I know he's out there," the Blackshirt commander said bitterly, grinding his yellowed teeth together. "That slime could be right up on those ridges at this moment," he mused aloud, staring the ten miles or so up to the lower slopes of the arching

Rocky Mountain peaks, ice tipped and shining in the dawn. Killov fingered the long scar that ran across the side of his face from just below the right eye to his lower jaw. A gift from Ted Rockson, who had kicked a glowing hot metal rod into his would-be torturer's face just when he himself was about to be branded. The wound was still red and throbbed at times, sending a streak of pain through Killov's central nervous system.

But the pain was good. For the colonel was a master of pain. And the burn scar, nearly an inch wide and a jagged eight inches long was a constant reminder of the power of pain. It made sure he would never forget. Someday he would get the "Ultimate American" as the rabble called him. It might take years, decades even, but he would *find* him—he would torture the man with the most exquisite pains the human body could experience. He wouldn't let Rockson die. No, death would be a kindness. The torture would be slow, days, weeks perhaps if his doctors could keep the rebel leader alive down in the subbasement of the Monolith filled with every pain-producing device known to man—even the new mind-breaking machine. Killov could picture the twin laser probes ripping into Rockson's skull. The sickly odor of the burning brain tissue—then the screams.

But first things first. It was Vassily and his idiot nephew Zhabnov whom Killov must deal with now. There had been two assassination attempts on the KGB commander's life within the last month. Both had failed. He was too clever, too quick for even the most highly trained assassins. But the Blackshirt leader knew there were more, and it added to his increasing paranoia. Everywhere were spies—no one was to be trusted. Anyone who entered his suite of rooms was searched and then had to walk through two detectors: one an x-ray device to pick up guns or knives; the other, an elemental spectrometer, to detect poisons and gases.

Killov rarely left the eightieth floor anymore. When he did, it was by helicopter which was stationed on the landing pad on the roof of the Monolith. But soon he wouldn't have to hide like this—like a cornered rat. They thought they had him now with their combined forces. But Killov knew he was a thousand times smarter than either of them. Already his own plots of counter-assassination were being planned. *They* would die—not he. Anyone who opposed him would be destroyed. He would rule. It was his destiny to be emperor of the planet, and then things would be done his way—as servant of the *Lord of Death*.

Chapter Six

"Jesus, Rock, look!" McCaughlin said, half tripping as he looked up toward immense clouds, each as big as a city, that flew quickly across the thick sky promising a downpour of rain over what had been the state of Montana. But it wasn't the clouds that had caught the Scotsman's eyes — it was the black dots that were approaching rapidly. Red choppers from the formation and speed — and they were coming right at the freefighters. Rockson, President Langford, Kim, and the rest of the Rock team had been moving carefully across some sparsely treed slopes to get the president back to his headquarters. They had traveled mostly at night to avoid the spy drones that now seemed to be everywhere. The Reds were still frantically searching for any survivors of the convention.

The Doomsday Warrior looked quickly around for any cover. He hoped the choppers hadn't seen them yet. Here, on the very top ridges of an almost barren mountain, they would be sitting ducks. If it had just been Rock and his crew, he wouldn't have felt so concerned—but with Kim and Langford along . . . If the Reds caught them all, they would have the biggest haul they had ever made. Medals and vodka would be flowing for months. His alert eyes saw the shadow of a cave several hundred yards down the decline ahead.

"Double time it," the Doomsday Warrior yelled out, wanting them all to feel the edginess in his voice. There was no time to play it cool. The party of Americans flew down the slope and into the dark spiderwebbed cavern. They all prayed that there were no grizzlies or other cave dwellers inside who would want to dispute ownership of the dark rock home. But a quick scan with a mini-flashlight by Chen showed nothing more than some bats seemingly unconcerned, hanging by the hundreds from the back roof of the nearly eighty-foot-deep cavern.

"Defensive alignment," Rock spat out and the team quickly went into one of their many battle modes that had been worked out and practiced for years. McCaughlin pulled out the folding fifty millimeter machine gun from its satchel over his right shoulder and moved it up to a low rock just inside the cave. Chen took eight of his exploding star knives from a hidden pouch inside his black ninja suit, fitting four into each hand.

Detroit tightened his grenade bandoliers that crisscrossed his linebacker-sized chest, taking off two of the metal pineapples and gripping them tightly in his black hands. Archer grumbled out an untelligible word or two and slipped his crossbow from around his back. He loaded it with an exploding arrow as he fit five more into the quickfire mechanism that he had built in just below the steel death-dealer. The team was ready—as ready as they'd ever be.

Rockson edged forward, pulling out his dust-coated field glasses and lifted them to the far sky. He saw what he feared: The choppers were coming straight ahead, right at the mountain peak. There were nearly twenty of them in a V-formation, big MS-20 jet helios, armed to the teeth with missiles, radar, and Rock knew from past experience nearly twenty elite combat troops in each, ready to drop down at a moment's notice on long nylon ropes. He could see the big Red stars on the sides—signifying Red Army. At least they weren't KGB. The regular army was usually a lot less enthusiastic about engaging in firefights with the freefighters.

But as the squadron of choppers continued unerringly on its straight course, Rock's heart began beating faster. They'd been seen—he could feel it. His sixth sense told him that some overzealous asshole aboard one of the craft had been looking through one of the super-scanners or perhaps one of the infrared scopes that could pick up any living thing for miles. The choppers would be upon them within a minute or two. Rock turned around, sliding back into the cave.

"We've got problems," he said, with a slightly sardonic grin. "Big problems." He glanced over at the pale Langford and Kim who looked back at the man she loved with big blue-green eyes, wide in fear and concern.

"We can take 'em, Rock," McCaughlin said. "Let me open up the fifty-five. If we can just get a few of the lead choppers the rest will pile up and—"

"Not this time, pal," Rock said. "There's too much at stake here. If President Langford should get captured, it would set our new government back for years, maybe decades. The morale of the freefighters would be dealt a heavy blow." The Doomsday Warrior had already made his decision. He knew they'd protest, but Rockson was the leader and there was nothing that would change his mind once it was made up. "We've got to create a diversion. They know there's someone here, but I'm sure they don't know how many or who. *I'm* going to be that diversion. It's our only chance. And I need someone with me—someone noticeable." He glanced over at Archer who had been listening intently to Rock's words. The near-mute who could utter only several words understood things perfectly. He grunted back at Rock.

"Archer—Archer come." The seven-foot-tall man had no fear of death or danger. Besides he owed his life to Rock who had saved him from a gruesome death in a quicksand pit.

"No Rock," Kim blurted out, jumping up and rushing over to him. "You can't go out there—you'll be—"

"I'm not ready to die yet, baby, I promise."

She flashed angry eyes at him. It was easier for him—he would just be gone—to wherever the dead go. She would be left alone, mourning for him, desiring him the rest of her life. She looked down at the moldy cave floor strewn with bat droppings and closed her eyes tightly, holding back the tears. There was nothing she could do, nothing she could say.

"Archer and I will make sure they see us. There's some woods down at the bottom of the far side of the mountain. If we can just get inside I'm sure we can loose them. Don't fire! You hear me. Sit tight! Don't do a thing, make a peep unless the bastards are actually coming into the cave." He looked at them sternly, knowing they were itching to get into the fray. "Get to the very back. If the Reds look in here and see nothing they probably won't even want to search. They hate dark places."

The men snickered. They all knew of the great courageous fighters of the Red Army — draftees who were zonked out on drugs half the time — just biding their time until they could head back to Mother Russia and out of this godforsaken land where everything was out to kill them.

"Give me some of your grenades," Rock said to Detroit. "Maybe we can do some jamming ourselves." Detroit quickly pulled off six of the hard-ball-sized explosives and handed them to the Doomsday Warrior. Archer walked over to him and slapped Rockson on the back, laughing with a grunt of disdain. "Kill!" Archer said. "Rock and Archer kill!" The rest of the team looked on in amazement. They had never seen the woods creature so loquacious.

"He's making a goddamned speech," Detroit

69

said with a smirk.

"Take care," Rock said, abruptly starting forward with the giant Archer at his side. He didn't look back. Kim reached forward involuntarily with outstretched arms and then quickly pulled them back, realizing how absurd the gesture was. A single tear formed in the corner of each eye. The Rock team pulled back into the innards of the cavern, lying on their stomachs behind a small drop in the cave floor. They shooed some bats away who moved, setting up sleeping quarters further up in the darkness. The freefighters lay stock-still, their weapons ready. The president and Kim were at the very edge of the back wall. The men would give their lives to protect them.

Out on the steep rocky slope the Doomsday Warrior and Archer began flying downhill. Rock knew there was no way the Red chopper sighters could miss a man as big as a goddamned ox. Archer took huge flying steps, landing every ten feet or so, while Rock took shorter more fluid steps, hardly sinking into the soft pebbly slope before jumping again. The choppers came in from the eastern sky like a swarm of hawks ready to draw blood. Their dim buzz turned into a deafening roar as the twenty helios beelined for the two moving figures.

"Don't fire yet," Commander Wilenski in the lead MS-20 ordered through his throat mike. "I want to see what we have here." The fleet of attack choppers which ironically had been heading toward a suspected Free City that one of their spies had reported, had just happened to catch the

70

freefighters' movement on their new Kinetic Scanner—one of the few recent technological innovations that Russia had produced—a device capable of picking up any motion over a certain kinetic energy at a range of up to twelve point five miles. The jet helicopters switched off their jet engines and went to rotor blades for lift. Their speed dropped within seconds from nearly three hundred fifty miles per hour to just under one hundred, then down to fifty. Slowly they zeroed in on their prey like a falcon descends on a rabbit.

Rockson turned around in motion and saw the twenty black engines of death just above the peak, coming in on him. Suddenly he dug his feet into the loose pebbles and stopped on a dime. He spun around and pulled the pins on two grenades. Archer, tearing down the slope like some sort of lumbering elephant, saw Rockson's plan and tried to stop himself the same way. He dug his heels in and flew face forward, traveling another twenty-five feet on his arms and stomach before he could stop. He jumped to his feet with a roar of humiliation and raised his crossbow. Rock released the first of the grenades, flinging his arm forward with the arc of a discus thrower. It soared into the sky straight up the mountainside. Archer sighted on the lead chopper and fired a three-foot-long steel shaft with a small charge of explosive plastique mounted on the tip. It shot through the air with an ominous whistle, moving at nearly two hundred fifty miles per hour.

The freefighters' weapons made contact with the fleet at the same instant. The grenade detonated just yards ahead of the forward copter, flaming grenade fragments ripping into the fifty-foot craft. A roar of metal turning to liquid and flesh to bloody mud screamed down the slope, sending rocks and pieces of glowing shrapnel in every direction. The chopper burst into a fireball as its munitions section detonated with the force of two tons of high explosive. The fireball reached out in all directions, an expanding circle of fire and metal as sharp as razors. The choppers immediately to the right and left of the leader took bad hits, both bursting into flame, then veering wildly down from the sky.

"Run!" Rockson screamed out above the thundering maelstrom above. Archer heard him and, after quickly slipping another arrow into its firing groove, took off after the Doomsday Warrior. The two freefighters catapulted down the rock-strewn hill toward the sheltering woods below. There were only yards to go. A hail of machine gun slugs ripped into the dirt just ahead of them, warning the two to stop or die. Rock pulled the pin from another grenade and used his forward motion to suddenly spin and, without looking, fling the sizzling pineapple backward, instantly taking off again. The pilot of the closest chopper saw the motion and twisted the metal bird to the right and up, trying to dodge the explosion. The grenade flew up just below the belly of the soaring Red chopper and went off. The brunt of the blast lifted straight up and into the bottom of the helio severing the fuel line. The MS-20, all ten tons of it, went up in an explosive puff of smoke, almost vaporizing the craft, so intense was the heat of the detonation. The choppers behind it flew forward, now under command of Captain Voshkov, having taken over from the lately deceased Wilenski who had died in the first explosion, Wilenski's craft just a pile of twisted metal wreckage near the top of the slope.

Rockson and the barn door of a man Archer hit the edge of the woods and tore into the shadows and leafy covering of the trees. We should have a chance in here, Rock thought as he and Archer zipped between the dark trees, ducking their heads beneath low branches. Rock couldn't help but smile even in the midst of fleeing the Reds. They had already taken out nearly a quarter of the fleet, and the Russians hadn't bothered to stop and check out the cave. His plan appeared to be working. Small forest creatures flew off around them, squealing and hiding in the thick twisted weeds of the forest as the two Americans ran as fast as their legs could carry them. The further they got from Kim and the president the better. Overhead they heard the loud whir of the copter engines. The Reds weren't about to give up so easily on this one.

Explosions went off about fifty yards behind them. Sounded like the crews were tossing grenades, just dropping them straight down as battleships of old would drop their explosive canisters to rouse hidden submarines. Rockson heard a loud thud to his right. Archer had caught a branch right in the face as he had turned to catch sight of the explosion lighting up the woods behind them. Rock stopped and reached a hand down for the

73

immense man in his oversized fatigues that were always ripping at the seams. Archer opened his eyes and saw Rockson looking down. He instantly realized how stupid he looked and smiled.

"Come on big fellow," the Doomsday Warrior said, helping the freefighter to his feet. "It happens to the best of us." The two of them once again hit cruising speed into the lengthening shadows as the sun began to fall lazily from the ocean-blue sky. Just a little more. Just let them not find us for another five minutes and we'll be free. Rock was sure of it. The thick trees of the surrounding mountains would make a perfect getaway for them. Ahead was a clearing, lit up with golden light from the warm rays of old Sol. It looked all right. Rockson stopped at the edge of the woods. About a hundred yards of lillies and daisies until the next patch of woods. The Reds seemed to be far behind them, still trying to flush them out.

"Come on." Rock raised his arm. "Fast!" The two men took off across the open field like jack-rabbits pursued by a fox. They had gone about thirty feet when the Doomsday Warrior heard a sound. Something? From above. They both dove to the ground as a large rope net dropped down from the trees. The net hit Archer, tangling his arms then his legs. He fell over on his side, roaring like a wild beast. Rock felt the net fall over his back, and he shot forward wriggling, avoiding entanglement. He reached the edge of it and came to his knees, pulling his .12 gauge shotpistol up ready to spit death.

"Please don't try that," a cold voice said. Rock

74

looked up. A Russian officer, a captain with a big red star on his brown cap, was holding a 9mm Special Service revolver aimed right between Rock's blue and violet eyes. On each side of the officer were nearly ten regulars, their Kalashnikovs pointed at the crouching American. Rock shrugged and let his pistol dangle from his fingers. He stood up slowly as troops tied the net around the furiously struggling Archer.

"Well, now, I may be mistaken," the mustached officer said with a sneer. "But this looks like the notorious Ted Rockson — the 'Ultimate American.' " He spat the words out contemptuously. "I've seen your picture enough on every brown wall in every military headquarters in this filthy country. You don't look so tough right now."

"Oh I'm not tough at all," Rock said smiling. "I'm just a pussycat. *He's* tough." Rock pointed down at the snarling and frantically flailing Archer who was trying to rip the net apart with brute strength, hard even for him, with two-inch cable totally surrounding his massive body. Rock's hands were cuffed behind his back, and he was marched into one of the choppers hidden in a second clearing beyond the next row of trees. Archer was carried in, still bound up in the net on a long metal pole, four men at each end.

"Looks like your fighting days are over, Rockson," the officer said needling him. "After Intel gets hold of you and puts you in one of those Mindbreakers, that I'm sure you've heard about, I don't think there'll be much left up there." He pointed to Rock's head with the muzzle of his pistol.

"Oh, yes, the Mindbreaker. I've already tried one, thank you," Rockson said through clenched teeth. "Quite a lot of fun. You should really take a spin in one yourself someday."

Half a mile behind them in the dusk of the now set sun, with jagged clouds passing overhead creating a maze of darkness below, the freefighters with Kim and the president slipped unnoticed down the back side of the mountain. Three choppers still burned just down the forward slope. Rock had done his job. God help him now.

Chapter Seven

The fleet of choppers pulled into their landing field at Fort Dobrynin near what had once been Chicago. But the Windy City had been hit with two twenty-megs and was now just a pair of immense craters filled with a swampy scum in which nothing grew. When the Reds had moved in a century earlier, they had built a fortress, one of the biggest in the Midwest about ten miles outside of the decimated metropolis swarming with cancer-ridden rats. The helicopters came to a full stop on a two-mile-long runway equipped to take even the Intercontinental Voyuz Stratojets that could carry up to five tanks in their gargantuan bellies. The needle-shaped control tower off to one side of the runway gave them directions, and they wheeled off to the special security sector of the field.

The Red Army command of the fortress had been radioed about the capture of the Doomsday

Warrior, and the entire complex was abuzz with excitement. If it was indeed Rockson, the top brass of the one hundred thousand man Russian force would all be sitting pretty. They marched out from the control tower, twenty of the highest officers, their uniforms pressed for the occasion, their rows of medals glittering on their chests, to personally direct the prisoners' entry into the fortress.

The freefighting mutant was taken from the lead chopper hands cuffed behind his back, steel shackles around his ankles. The Red captain who was now in command of the attack force had heard too many stories of the man's uncanny ability to escape every Russian trap that had been set for him to allow even the slightest opportunity. It would be his head for sure if Rockson made a getaway. A dozen Red troops stood around their prisoner, subs aimed at his chest and back. There was no way in hell he was going to get out of this one. Archer was another story. The man was too big and too strong to even shackle. He looked as if he could snap chains with his teeth. The captain decided to keep him in the netting, screaming his version of curses: animal growls ands grunts.

The Red command stood about fifty feet from the slowly spinning rotors of the choppers and smiled broadly as Rockson was marched up to them.

"So it is you, after all," the top commander of the fortress, General Pushkin said. "We weren't really sure they had captured you." He held a large wanted poster up next to Rockson's face with the words Wanted Dead Or Alive, 500,000 rubles Reward written on it below a sketched drawing of Ted Rockson, and then looked again at the Doomsday Warrior. "Unmistakable — the white streak down the middle of the head — the mismatched eyes — only one man could look like that."

"If I'd known I was so famous I would have given an autograph party long ago," Rock said, spitting the words in the general's face.

"Guard him well," Pushkin snarled to the guards. "And don't harm a hair on his mutant head — this man is worth his weight in plutonium." The brass watched with smug grins as the Doomsday Warrior was marched past them and into the large debriefing room just to the other side of the airport fence.

The intelligence chief, Colonel Pastrok, sat at a large wooden table with a single chair on the other side. The guards pushed Rockson roughly down, one of them hitting him with the butt of his Kalashnikov on the freefighter's shoulder.

"Name?" the colonel asked with a false smile. He offered the American a cigarette from a Russian pack — *Sputnik* filters.

"John Doe," Rock answered. "And I don't smoke except from a gun."

"Come now, we know you're Ted Rockson. Let's not play games with one another." The interrogator's face had a silver dollar-sized purple birthmark on the left cheek which contrasted sharply with his otherwise pasty flesh. His eyes narrowed as he spoke. "The more you cooperate the less painful it will be for you. That I promise you — as an officer of the Imperial Russian Army."

"I trust you Reds as far as I can sight my rifle," Rock said dryly. "There are graveyards of Americans who listened to your bull. I've seen too much to even think of cooperation. Why don't you just kill me and get it over with. Otherwise I might just escape from here."

"Kill you." The officer laughed. "Oh no, Mr. Rockson, that will never do. You're in for quite an extended period of interrogation. Or should I use the less glamorous term—torture. When we can get inside that mutant head of yours I'm sure we'll find out wonders—not to mention the location of half the Free Cities in this hellhole of a country. Your capture may well signal the beginning of the end for your rebel forces. Take him away for now," he commanded the guards. "Put him in Maximum Security Cell Three. I don't want any other prisoners anywhere near him. Clear out the whole block. Just have this Rockson and that foul-smelling creature that was captured with him put in there. Separate cells. I want ten armed guards in there at all times. This man is not what you would call a normal prisoner."

"I'm touched," Rockson said. The Doomsday Warrior knew that his chance for escape would come—not now—but it would come. They would make a slip, be lax for just one moment, and Rockson would move. He was marched down a long hallway and taken by elevator down to one of many cellblocks in the military prison. Even through the thick walls he could hear the screams of other prisoners. The Reds seemed to love the sound of pain—it was music to their ears. He was pushed into a cell and the steel-barred door slammed shut behind him, locking with a loud click. The guards stepped back, and the chief of security leveled his Tokarev .65 pistol at Rock's head.

"As long as you're here, don't try anything. I'd rather shoot you than let you escape. You understand? I won't hesitate. I can never let you escape. Never!"

"I'm scared," Rock quipped through the inch-thick steel bars. "I promise, cross my heart, to be good." The Doomsday Warrior looked around his cell—solid as they come. A video camera on the ceiling swung slowly around, transmitting pictures of every foot of the cell and its occupant to technicians in a control booth several floors above. Man, they really weren't taking any chances with him. Rock heard a noise, a moan, and rushed forward against the bars. About thirty feet down the cell-block Archer was coming to. They had apparently shot him full of drugs before daring to release him from the netting. The huge man stood up wobbly and saw Rock. A smile crossed his black-bearded face.

"Rockssssssonnnn," he howled. He seemed overjoyed that Rock was still alive. Archer had a kind of magical belief in the Doomsday Warrior's ability to survive. If Rock was around—anything was possible.

They were fed after a few hours, not too tasty, but food nevertheless. Rockson wondered if it were drugged but then shrugged his shoulders and ate the meat and potato stew down. Whatever they were going to do — they would do. Archer gobbled down his helping in seconds and held the bowl out through the bars for more. The food dribbled down over his dark beard but he took no notice. The Reds looked on in disgust as if at a savage. Which he probably, was Rock thought. But he'd take savages like Archer, who, in spite of his appearance, had more of a code of ethics and honor than any Russian in the whole damned country.

Several hours passed, with the guards smoking cigarettes and playing cards at a small table in the center of the corridor that ran past the rows of green-painted cells. At last another officer came in, a dark-complexioned man with almost platinum-white hair. He was accompanied by a dozen armed guards.

"You," he said, pointing to Rockson. "Time for some fun." Rock was led from the cell still in his cuffs and leg chains. Archer let out a roar of protest. Suddenly he felt alone, frightened, and paced the cell wildly, pulling at the bars with all his strength, making the entire side of the cell vibrate violently. The guards stepped back knowing he couldn't — but somehow afraid that the seven-foot freefighter with the huge black eyes could rip his prison cell apart. They pulled back the safeties on their rifles and looked at one another nervously.

Rockson was marched through several long brightly lit hallways to a large room filled with what were obviously torture implements. A white-smocked man stood rubbing his hands together in delighted anticipation of the time they were about to spend together.

"Ah, Mr. Rockson, so glad you could make our little party," the technician of pain said. Although his neck-to-ankle smock had been washed and bleached, Rock could see flecks of pale red: blood from the torturer's past victims.

"And I'm so glad I could come," Rock said, his blue and violet eyes cold as tempered steel. "I hope I'm not too late. Have all the guests left?"

"There's always room for one more," the flabby technician of pain said with a smile of his thick blubbery lips. "Please do be seated." The guards brusquely threw Rockson down on a long board and cuffed his hands to hooks on each side. Rock breathed out deep, going into a semi-meditative trance where his mind could detach from the pain his body would feel. He felt no fear. Just a longing for Kim—to touch her soft skin—taste her lips one more time before leaving the world of the living.

"Now, what kind of pain would you like to begin with? An appetizer as it were or the main course?" the pale technician asked in a low voice. "Somehow I feel that tonight we should give you a demonstration of the full range of our—accessories." He snapped his fingers at two of his assistants similarly attired in the gray smocks, pointing to a long whip across the room. It hung on a wall which was filled with every type of crude instrument of pain from bullwhips to hammers, knives to scalpels, masks with spikes inside of them, bludgeons, needles, and shiny mechanical devices that looked quite incomprehensible and quite dangerous.

"Whips are *so* old-fashioned," the torturer said in apology, "but they do hurt." He took the cat-o-nine-tails lined with small razor-sharp spikes only about a quarter of an inch long. "These are special—made of—oh well, why talk about it when it can so easily be demonstrated." The short, squat Red pain tech pulled the whip back and then swung it forward with all his might across Rockson's back. Hundreds of small metal teeth ripped through the Doomsday Warrior's khaki shirt and into his flesh, making scores of small razor cuts. But the mutant skin didn't bleed. The cuts had not reached his protected arterial and nervous system set inside the skin nearly half an inch deeper than the average Homo Sapien's. Still, the pain was intense. Rockson pulled his consciousness up from his body into his mind. He was floating—floating free of the physicality that was Ted Rockson. The cat-o-nine bit into the broad muscular back again and again, cutting the shirt to tatters. Cuts covered the Doomsday Warrior's flesh, and at last blood began creeping out through gashes that had been torn two or three times.

"Ah, I've struck paydirt have I?" The torture tech laughed with a satisfied snort. His jowls of waxy dough rippled in flesh waves beneath the stubbly chin. The man enjoyed his work.

"Has the party begun?" Rock asked, his face pressed against the blood-soaked board.

"I'm bored with this," the torture tech snapped angrily, wanting Rockson to grovel beneath him. He tossed the now red whip to one of his assistants who caught it and returned it to the wall. "Bring me the prod—yes the prod will make a nice main course." The assistant took down a long cylindrical-shaped device and brought it over to Rock's tormentor who turned a dial on the pain machine up to the red—danger—level.

"I don't see why we should waste time with preliminaries." He smirked at his victim, lying still below him. "I'll just set it at maximum and see what we can get out of you." He placed the tip of the amplified electric cattle prod at the small of Rock's back. The muscles in the Doomsday Warrior tightened into knots of pain, his back arching upward and jerking spasmodically. He felt the pain, but as an object, an illusion, and did not let it take his spirit.

"Mary had a little lamb," Rock muttered over his shoulder. The torture tech reached forward again, this time touching the shiny tip of the electric spike just below the base of Rock's neck. Again, pain, like a lightning bolt, surging through him. His head rocketed back and forth on his neck like some kind of bouncing doll out of control. He was in another place, another dimension where the normal laws of the body no longer applied. He placed himself beyond pain and stood back as one might watch a movie of one's own death. The torturer pulled the prod back and glared down at his captive.

"And its fleece was white as snow," Rock spat out through clenched teeth. Maybe if he could make the pain dealer angry enough he'd make a mistake and kill him. The days, weeks, of torture would be destroyed—all the information they hoped to get from Rock—gone in the corpse of his body. Rockson would get the last laugh yet.

"Hey I hear most of you pain freaks get your kicks from raping dead babies. Is it true?" the Doomsday Warrior asked his torturer through a blue haze of pain. The tech's face grew red as an overripe beet, and he slammed the prod down against Rock's head, hitting the Doomsday Warrior on the back of the skull full force. The blow Rock absorbed easily—then came the electricity directly into his brain. The pain was unbelievable. Even he couldn't escape it now. It filled every fiber of his consciousness, every path he turned to escape. A low groan fell from his white lips. The torture tech held the device against Rock's skull for nearly ten seconds, when one of the Red Army officers present jumped up shouting.

"Don't kill him, you fool, or it's *your* life, too!" The tech pulled the prod angrily away and looked down at his prisoner. Rockson let his senses settle back into their proper modes and then opened his eyes, staring up at the expert of pain.

"Is that all?" he managed to whisper out. "I must admit I'm disappointed. Why little girls from the Free Cities could take this much. There must be something more."

"Yes, Mr. Rockson. Yes indeed, there is something more. Something of a whole different dimension." He turned to his two assistants and snapped his fingers together with the sharp sound of a branch cracking. "Bring it in." The two under-assistant torture technicians rushed through a side door and quickly reappeared pushing a large oval-shaped fiberglass chair with a blinking device on the top with the appearance of a streamlined diving helmet.

"Oh, I've heard of these," Rock said lifting up slightly from the board. "That's one of those Mindbreakers. Everyone's been raving about them. Do wonders for the hair. The women in my Free City give themselves permanents every morning with one of these."

"You're a fool, Rockson," the torturer muttered through grinding teeth. "In minutes you'll tell us everything and anything we want to know. I guarantee you." The guards uncuffed the Doomsday Warrior and half carried him toward the chair. He glanced around—guns were trained on him from every direction. There wasn't a chance. They quickly tied him into the black shiny seat and lowered the helmet from which dropped two steel prongs tipped with rubies that would soon emit pinpoint laser beams that would burn into his skull.

"First they vaporize the skull bone itself, Mr. Rockson. Then they rip into the brain tissue erasing all memories of loyalty—of friend or enemy. We know just the right sections to burn out. And it hurts. It hurts horribly. Or so I've been told." He laughed loudly and looked around at his two assistants who quickly joined in shrill, cackling sounds. The torturer retreated about two yards away, reaching a hand toward a control panel on the wall to which the Mindbreaker had been wired.

Suddenly the black phone on a far desk rang loudly. "I told them to cut that damned thing off," Intel Chief Pastrok yelled. He rushed over and picked up the receiver screaming into the mouthpiece.

"Who the hell is this? Don't you know we're—" Someone on the other end said something back and the officer's face turned white as a sheet. "Yes sir. Yes sir. Immediately sir. Absolutely. Yes sir!" He hung up the phone and turned around, his shoulders hanging limply in their sockets. Suddenly he saw the torture tech's hand on the laser activation switch.

"Stop! Stop!" He ran over and ripped the man's hand from the controls.

"What are you doing?" the greasy-faced tech protested. "I'm in charge here—"

"You fool. That was General—I mean—President Zhabnov on the phone. He knows Rockson's here and wants him immediately flown to Washington. He said, if there's a mark on his body, we'll all pay." The gathered officers and the torture crew looked at one another nervously and then at Rockson. They quickly released him from the chair, pulling the Mindbreaker up away from his head.

"Sorry about that," the chief whispered with a wild look on his face. "The—the—president wants to see you."

"Thanks so much for this little get-together," Rock said, sitting up and rubbing the back of his skull with his hand. "I'll remember—all of you—always."

Chapter Eight

President Zhabnov sat inside his embattled White House, his manicured hands resting on the cherry table before him, as he stared across at Rockson, the "Ultimate American," about whom he had heard so much. He glanced nervously over at the giant mutant man, the foul-smelling mumbling Archer who was seated between four guards of the elite White House Legion. He was damned lucky to get these two. He had heard rumors that Colonel Killov had once had Rockson in his grasp deep within Pavlov City's basement dungeons, and that the man had escaped, after scarring Killov horribly on the face. Zhabnov rubbed his cheek nervously — he didn't like the idea of scars — not on his white sensitive skin. He tried to stare Rock down, staring into the fierce icy mismatched eyes of violet and aquamarine set in the center of the rugged, chiseled tan face. Then he turned away, unable to bear the stronger will of the prisoner. The president waited for Rock to speak and when he didn't, at last spoke himself.

"Welcome to the capitol, Ted Rockson."

"The American capitol is now out West," Rock answered bitterly.

"Ah yes, that is what you rebels say. *Where,* Rockson? Where is this so-called Century City?"

"That would take the fun out of your little treasure hunt—if I told you."

"Ah yes, your anti-response technique, hypnoplanted by your scientists," Zhabnov said, leaning forward on the shiny wood table.

"The worms crawl in, the worms crawl out," Rockson answered drolly.

"Admirable, admirable. You are shot full, my assistants tell me, of paralyzing mind drugs that would make any of *us* talk, blabber in fact, and yet you bear the effect and even manage to spit out your concept of humor—fascinating. I intend to study this brain of yours—perhaps have my scientists dissect—" The red phone at the edge of the White House table began to blink on and off, under the portrait of John F. Kennedy. The president reached over. "Excuse me gentlemen," he said and lifted the receiver. It was Premier Vassily.

"Your Excellency," Zhabnov stuttered, his mouth instantly dry.

"Yes, yes," the voice on the other end said brusquely, "let's dispense with the formalities, nephew." Nephew—that was a good sign.

"Yes, Grandfather—and to what do I owe the pleasure of hearing your voice?"

90

"I understand you have stumbled upon some good luck. You have captured Rockson—correct?"

"Grandfather, through diligent, meticulous investigation and the full committment of my forces, I have indeed captured, at great losses, the famous—"

"Yes, yes, nephew," Vassily cut him off. "What *luck*. Where is he?"

"Here, Your Excellency. They are being probed with SA-seventy-seven drugs for information as to the whereabouts of their famous Century City but—"

"Yes, I know, the hypno-blocking. They recite nursery rhymes. Don't bother me with details—and don't hurt him."

"Excellency?" Zhabnov said nervously, looking over at his prisoners who listened with interest to the conversation of the two most powerful men in the world.

"I said don't hurt them. Feed them well, take them off the mind drugs. I want them flown over here to Moscow. To the Kremlin within twenty-four hours."

"But—but—"

"Get them over here—and quick," the premier snapped. "There have been changes in the world situation—for the worse—fighting is going on everywhere. If a truce of some sort could be worked out with these annoying American freefighters, we could deploy some of your forces elsewhere and give more of our time to countering that madman Killov."

"Redeploy my forces—but—" Zhabnov sud-

91

denly had a sinking feeling in the pit of his large stomach. His power could be greatly diminished if his troops were cut. Was this the beginning of the end for him?

"Stop repeating every word I say, nephew. Do as I say. I'll put Rahallah on the phone and he will arrange the details of the transfer of this Rockson and his fellow rebel to Moscow. Rahallah is more than my servant now—he is a trusted advisor."

"A *nigger*? Trust a *nigger*—but Grandfather, how—"

"Don't use that word, nephew. You are making me grow angry. Do as I command. I have a good future planned for you. Since Killov has rebelled you are the one most likely to succeed me now. And I am old." He sounded weary. resigned. "But I must have your unquestioned obedience until then. And you must accept Rahallah like a brother. He saved my life. Do you understand me?"

Zhabnov nearly choked when he answered, "Yes, Your Excellency. Thank you for your confidence. I will have matters of transfer arranged. Please put—brother—Rahallah on." He handed the phone to General Smayok and turned back to face Rockson whose keen mutant ears had picked up much of the conversation.

Rockson was being tossed around like a hot potato. Just when his future seemed so bleak—very interesting. Of course being in Russia would be even more difficult to get out of than here. But the possibilities—the possibilities. . . . Suddenly he was enjoying his capture tremendously.

Chapter Nine

A DAY IN THE LIFE OF IVAN KRESKY

Ivan Kresky rolled over in the soft dirt ditch he had spent the night sleeping in. The cold dew of the morning was beginning to evaporate with the arrival of the dark orange sun which hoisted itself slowly into the mottled Russian sky over the Red city of Petrograd, home of nearly six million. Kresky shivered from the wetness which covered him, and he pulled his one miserable possession, an ancient army overcoat, brown and encrusted with dirt, up over his body. He withdrew his head deep into his little cave of relative warmth underneath the blanketlike embrace of the coat. And tried not to wake up. There was nothing to wake up to. Nothing. Around him, Kresky heard the muffled moans of other dulags—untouchables— as the Russians called them. They lived on the outskirts of every Soviet city. Inside the city — the bureaucrats, the army brass, all lived plush lives surrounded by all the wealth that the World Soviet Empire sucked in with its long greedy tentacles. But the other seventy-five percent of the Russian population even within their own country were not so lucky. Many of them were poor farmers, eking what meager existence they could from their rocky acres. Others worked in the Russian factories turning out yet more tanks, trucks, military supplies to keep the empire troops supplied. For the fighting continued — even after a hundred years. The conquered peoples didn't seem to want to give up their freedom so easily. Father taught son who taught his son to fight. To kill Russians whenever the opportunity arose.

But a vast portion of the Russian population didn't even have factory or agricultural livelihoods at all. Nearly forty million of her citizens were forced to fend for themselves, living off the upper classes' wealth, trying to grab what little crumbs they could to keep themselves alive. Without homes they wandered the countryside in search of God knows what. Sleeping in woods, behind logs, in ditches, then rising again each morning in pursuit of scraps thrown from the cities. They scoured the immense garbage dumps at the outskirts of the Red metropolises, fighting the rats and the worms and one another for the few precious rotting mouthfuls.

Ivan had been born in the Siberian village of Moersk, a small hunting community in the southern Steppes where the winters were nine months long and there were few days when one could take one's shirt off and bask in the brief sunshine. But there were fewer and fewer game animals to hunt. The poisoning of the Russian ecology by the handful of American nukes that made it over had not initially caused much damage, but over the years they had made their effects felt as the ecological harmony of the precarious life forms in many parts of frozen Russia had been pushed over the edge into extinction. Nearly half of all Soviet wildlife had disappeared in the fifty years following the Great War. Much of the flora that had covered the mountains and Steppes had vanished, leaving parched flat plains without a trace of life. The small outer villages were doomed. Slowly they shrank as their once proud and robust inhabitants became bent and thin, hardly able to catch enough game to keep their families from starving.

Ivan, the fifth son of Strydor Kresky, had set off from home at the ripe age of fourteen — or rather been kicked out bodily by his stern, vodka-drinking father who had grown tired of all the mouths to feed. When his wife had twins it had been the door for Ivan — literally kicked out into the snow with just the boots on his feet, a thick black bear coat and a rusty pistol. Somehow Ivan had survived, trekking south before the worst of winter set in. He had slept by the sides of roads, lonely and desperate, happy just to hear the occasional Ziv Army car fly by, happy for a split second for his speeding company in the midst of the vast Russian wastelands.

He had headed west to the center of the Motherland falling in among the migrating hordes who hopped trains and built rickety rafts to move up and down the mighty Volga, always searching, seeking, but none knew for what.

But the years of constant struggle had taken a heavy toll on him. He was only twenty-five but looked like a man of fifty, his face lined and weathered, his eyes fixed in narrow, suspicious slits hardly larger than a razor's edge. He had numerous wounds and sores, scars from fights with other dulags battling over this or that crumb tossed out by the elite. A bullet was still lodged in his side from a Red guard who had shot him for target practice one night as he was going through a metal dumpster parked at the edge of a city. His flesh was filled with wounds from the teeth of life, teeth that never stopped snapping.

Ivan heard engines roaring by on the road about thirty feet away from where he lay. The traffic of early morning was beginning to move in and out of Petrograd, delivery trucks from outlying warehouses bringing in the foodstuffs and materials that had been stolen from other parts of the globe. Ninety-seven percent of the earth's population spent their short lives working for and producing goods so that three percent of the Russian population could live in ultimate luxury. Never had so many given so much for so few.

Ivan sat upright, letting his thick army coat fall to his waist. All around him in the shallow ditch in which he had spent the night other dulags were rousing themselves. It wasn't good to be seen sleeping when the army brass went by. They were just as likely to run the prone untouchable over or shoot them with a machine gun, laughing uproariously. The poorest of the poor stood up on unsteady legs and looked at one another suspiciously. There were many of them in this particular area. There had been rumors that there was work to be had in the textile mills at the edges of the city, and thousands of them had come, some vast distances, to see if it was true—a job. A real job, and perhaps a dwelling—even a hovel would have seemed a castle to these nothings—these nobodies.

"Food," one of the dulags, an old man with a face covered with brown warts, groaned just behind Ivan. The man was trembling violently, his hands reaching out ahead of him, palms up as if God were about to drop a feast down on them. Ivan looked over at him with eyes as cold as the frozen tundra. He had seen so much suffering, death, disease, that he was immune to it. The human system can only take so much before it goes into a state of shock—before a numbness sets in through which nothing can any longer be felt. The old man screamed once more for food, and with a thick green bile dribbling between his lips, keeled over face forward onto the hard cushion of gravel at the edge of the road.

"We die like flies," a large, barrel-chested man who had slept just behind Ivan said angrily. "We are nothing. We are the no-people."

"I am hungry," a thin, gaunt man off to the side of the road cried out. "I've had no food for days. I can't remember when."

"Yes, I am hungry, too," Ivan said, joining in

the growing chorus of angry voices. Suddenly there was a group of dulags, then a crowd, voicing their discontent, their anger. For years they had remained dormant, silent, dead. But now, a breaking point had been reached. Even the lowliest slave can only be pushed so far.

"We are all dying," the big man said. It was obvious that he had once been very strong. His big bones and broad chest were testimony to a peasant of tremendous strength — a cow lifter as the Russians termed that kind of strength. Yet now his flesh and muscles hung loosely on his large frame. He was wasting away — as they all were wasting away. Men turning into nothing.

Food, I must have food," an old man with white beard that came nearly down to his waist, croaked out. "I am ready to die for food."

"Yes, we must eat," the voices echoed around him. There were nearly a hundred of the dulags now, roused from their sleeping nooks by the angry sounds of so many voices. Their eyes lit up for the first time in years. Just to hear the anger, the dissatisfaction, made their hearts swell, brought up the bitter juices of hate that had been hidden for so long deep inside them.

"They must give us food — today," the large man said, clothed in a torn flannel shirt with one of the sleeves missing. He had no shoes on his feet, just thick weeds wrapped round and round the swollen heels and toes. "They have so much — we have nothing. Nothing!" He screamed out the words in defiance.

"Nothing," they echoed back, their voices growing louder by the second.

"Come, we go now," he said. He had become their leader. They who were without leaders suddenly had one in their midst, and the rebellion in his voice fueled them like gasoline poured into a fire. They marched forward, their rags hanging down around them, torn pants flapping over thin legs. They walked onto the road and toward the city. They were in a state of madness, uncaring of what their fate would be. Death, if it came, could only be a friend to those who had nothing. As they walked along the road they shouted at the other untouchables sleeping everywhere out in the open, to join them. The sleepy men roused themselves, amazed at the rebellious crowd, marching with their heads held high, their eyes flaming with righteous anger. They had never seen any such uprising before. They had no words to describe it. Just feelings, deep in their guts. Feelings of power, of strength — something unknown but weirdly beautiful.

The crowd grew as it marched along the dirt road which turned to paved highway about two miles from the main entrance to Petrograd. Their fury gave them strength. It surged through their starving bellies, filled their tired limbs with the electric energy of those who fight back.

Suddenly an army staff car came zipping down the paved road toward them. The two officers in the back seat could hardly believe their eyes as they took in the marching mob before them.

"Stop!" the young lieutenant yelled to the driver. The car screeched to a halt just ahead of the now nearly six hundred dulags. The officer took out his Tokarev .65 clip loaded revolver and held it straight in front of him as he stood up in the open-topped vehicle.

"Where the hell do you think you're going?" he screamed out with the contempt of the Russian command.

"Food, we need food," the leader yelled from the front of throngs. "We are hungry. We are human beings. We deserve more than scraps."

"You deserve nothing," the young officer said, standing tall in his crisply pressed uniform. "We decide what is given. Now disperse back to your wretched holes before you all die." He fired a shot over their heads. Many of the untouchables cowered, pulling their heads down, diving to the ground. But not the leader and those who stood with him in the mob's front ranks.

"This time you cannot frighten us with your toys," the big man said, pulling a large curved dagger from the back of his mud-coated gray pants. "You are the ones who are going to die." Others in the mob also pulled their weapons from their sleeves and pockets: knives, pieces of glass, ice-picks, meathooks. All had killed before. Their own. But now it would feel good to kill those who had enslaved them, destroyed them. They started toward the car.

The lieutenant grew pale. They weren't supposed to act like this. He had never seen the dulags do anything more than cower. His power of authority seemed to crumble around his suddenly frail-looking body. He aimed at the leader and fired. The shot caught the leader in his right shoulder but he didn't flinch. He laughed and spat at the ground as he came forward.

"I have survived much worse than that fool." The driver slammed the car into reverse and stepped on the accelerator, but before he had gone a yard the mob was upon the army vehicle. They grabbed the sides and lifted it, quickly tipping it over. The wheels spun uselessly in the air. The mob fell upon the three Red officers, stabbing at them, flailing away with their crude but efficient weapons. Within seconds the soldiers were bloody carcasses lying in the road, blood pouring from a hundred wounds.

The death of the Reds emboldened the small army of untouchables. They raised their arms and roared out screams of defiance. Never had they felt like this—like men. Several of them sawed away at the corpses and quickly butchered the heads free from the bodies. They found branches at the side of the road and speared them into the bloody appendages. They held the three heads high—their flag of conquest. Now they marched forward even faster. Anger, hate, murder in every step. More and more of the dulags joined them, streaming out from their hiding places in trees, under bridges, behind bushes. Within a mile their number had grown to nearly a thousand and continued increasing at every step. They came upon four more army cars and quickly disposed of the inhabitants, losing several of their own in the skirmishes.

But they were no longer afraid. The taste of blood was maddening—they wanted more. They came to the very edge of the city. Huge gates stood open at each side of the main entrance several hundred feet away. The twenty or so guards, lounging around the front, stared at the approaching army of the untouchables with eyes as big as moons. They never had any trouble with the rabble other than a few incidents of thieves grabbing at a gun or lunging at a soldier—and being quickly disposed of. The officer in charge ran to a phone just inside the entrance and frantically called central command.

"We're being attacked," he screamed out.

"What? What the hell are you talking about?" the officer at the other end asked in a bored tone, wondering if the gate guard had been drinking again.

"We're being *attacked*, you idiot. There must be a thousand of them. They're right here at the gate."

"Who? Who? the desk officer asked, suddenly alarmed.

"The dulags. I know it sounds incredible but—" His voice was cut off as a thrown knife whirled through the air and caught him in the back. The officer fell to the concrete ground, the phone dropping from his hand. The front ranks of the dulags tore into the gate troops. Within seconds twenty torn bodies lay in pools of hot blood, their eyes wide, their mouths contorted in screams of sheer horror. The heads were again sliced clean from the corpses and mounted atop poles. The head bearers marched at the front, into the city, walking through a large open area that was sometimes used as an outdoor market, still largely empty in the early morning. The peddlers who were just starting to set up their vegetable and used goods stands stood stock-still in amazement at the vision of the army moving forward, forty heads now held aloft on blood-splattered pikes.

"Join us, men who are nothing. Join us or die!" the leader yelled. The peddlers ran in terror toward a second gate at which Red troops were now setting up machine guns. As the peddlers came toward the inner gate they were mowed down like so many rats, falling by the bloody dozens onto the concrete square. The dulag army surged forward screaming as they charged at the line of defense.

"Food, give us food—bread, meat. Give us food or die." The troops opened up on the advancing ragtag army, taking out nearly fifty of the forward ranks in just seconds. But still the untouchable came forward, no longer afraid of anything. Death was a joke to them now. Blood was what they wanted. If they could not eat bread, then they would taste Red Army blood. The officer in charge of the second line saw that they would be overrun within minutes. Already the ranks were shouting at one another, getting ready for another charge.

"Close the gate," he bellowed, a large-paunched sergeant with muscular arms and thighs. "Pull back." The machine gunners dragged their tripod-mounted 55mm back several yards as the officer slammed his fist onto the buttons that controlled the motion of the two towering steel gates. The nearly thirty-foot high, two-inch thick steel doors whirred swiftly along ball bearing tracks and slammed shut with a resounding bang that echoed through the square.

The army of no-men looked around. Who could they kill now? They ran through the large open space, grabbing the food the dead peddlers had dropped as they ran.

"Food, food—see, we have won our dinner," one of the headholders cried out. They forgot their weapons and even their whereabouts, so intense was their hunger. They pounced on the fresh fruits, the flaky pies, and loaves of bread piled high atop round wooden tables. They didn't even notice a squad of Russian soldiers silently close the front gates as well. After they had gorged themselves, gobbling down the feast by the handful, slamming it into their thin, starving mouths, they looked around, suddenly remembering their situation and the trouble that might ensue.

"We leave now," the leader said, still bleeding from the shot that had caught him in the shoulder. "We have won! Now we go back to hills—we hide." He held one of the heads high, moving it up and down high above his arms, an insane flag of Red death.

Suddenly they heard a sound above them—choppers—three of them roaring over the square. The army of dulags, clutching every bit of food they could carry, rushed toward the front gate. The first to reach it found it locked tight and they screamed out.

"We're trapped. The bastards have trapped us." The untouchables ran off in every direction, their cohesion and unity broken by the sudden realization that *they* were about to be victims. They spread out over the nearly six-square-acre marketplace like roaches fleeing for their very lives. The helicopter gunships came in from one end of the square, flying slowly about seventy-five feet apart. The twin machine guns in their bellies opened up, sending a hail of 55mm slugs down whistling murder. The chopper guns were capable of firing nearly five thousand rounds a minute. They tore into the dulag mob like the Angel of Death. The huge slugs tore right through the bodies of the untouchables, some of them taking ten, twenty of the three-inch-long bullets in their bodies. They were ripped to shreds as arms, lungs, faces, and hearts were blasted right out of their human containers.

It didn't take very long. The glass slivers and knives and hooks of the dulags were hardly a match for the death-dealing high-tech weaponry of the Red helios. The vast, screaming crowd was peppered with tens of thousands of rounds. The concrete around the falling bodies was ripped apart in little explosions of dust as the cartridges created countless little craters between the falling bodies.

When the helicopters reached the far end of the square they turned quickly and came back again, sending down a deluge of death. Within two minutes of their initial appearance over the walls not a dulag moved. All were dead. All were not recognizable as men any longer. Their bodies had been blown into a bloody swamp of crumbling flesh which covered the entire square. Not a moan, not a single breath stirred the smoky air. The army of untouchables was now an army of the dead.

Chapter Ten

The two captured freefighters were whisked up the aisle of the huge Illyushin-78 Ramjet and told to make themselves comfortable. There were nearly two hundred seats inside but only they, a dozen guards, and the plane crew got aboard. The stewardesses were bulky Russian women in drab gray suits and low black shoes with their stern potatolike faces. The stewardesses strapped Rock and Archer into their seats at the tail section of the plane. The guards sat in front, behind, *and* in the seats on each side of them. They were taking no chances.

It was a gut-wrenching takeoff, and it felt as if the jet went nose up the second it left the runway, not leveling off until it reached the stratosphere after about five minutes. The ear-splitting roar of the engines died somewhat as they hit the thinner air high above the earth and caught into the global jet stream. The chunky stewardesses brought them tasty caviar spreads and sandwiches without crusts and good thick rich Columbian coffee, black as a pit. Archer picked up five of the tiny sandwiches at a time and swallowed them down without apparently tasting their delicate subtle flavors from around the world. Rock savored each bite — better than the slop they'd been given in the prison. He still felt a bit weak from the aftereffects of his little pain session. But Archer seemed just fine. After a few loud burps and one fart that threatened to make the guards retreat to the far end of the plane, the big primitive fellow fell asleep, his head plopping down onto Rockson's shoulder, and he began snoring like a bull elephant.

Rockson was looking forward to the meeting with the Grandfather, wondering just what the cagey premier had in mind. He was intrigued that Vassily had a black servant — with some power — how odd. The man was also, rumor stated, of above average intelligence and read profusely. He knew from his sources that Vassily was of late locked in a struggle to the death with Colonel Killov to maintain his power over who ran America. Suddenly Rock realized the reason for the trip: to be used by Vassily to defeat Killov. But two could play that game, and Rockson was an ace at no-rules poker.

The steel curtains over the windows rolled back, and Rock nearly gasped as he took in the view below. They were in goddamned space itself. They were, Rock guessed, nearly twenty miles up, and the curve of the horizon above which stars dotted the sky was slow and beautiful. He had known the Ramjets flew high but this . . .

"Mmmm," Archer groaned, suddenly rising and unsnapping his seat belt. The guards leaped up, leveling their pistols and Kalashnikovs at the giant, but Archer pointed to his groin and made a pained face.

"I think he wants to use your gentlemen's facilities," Rock said.

The Red guards motioned Archer forward but as he took a step, much to his astonishment, he began slowly floating up toward the cushioned ceiling, banging his head. He flailed his arms and kicked his long legs frantically as ifs trying to swim through the weightless air.

"Relax buddy," Rock said, grabbing an elephantine ankle and pulling gently down until Archer reached his seat. The Red guard came over and gave them each a set of shoes with magnetic bottoms. Archer put his on, not quite able to close even the largest pair, and began, nimbly for him, walking up the aisle looking sick as a dog.

"How high are we?" Rock asked one of his guards.

"Twenty-eight miles," the beefy soldier answered proudly. "Flying about seven times the speed of sound at ground level. Five thousand miles per hour. We are in free fall, as you say." Rock heard the toilet flush and wondered if Archer's huge deposit was now a meteor about to flash across the sky of the north pole. The Doomsday Warrior unhooked himself under their careful gaze — why they bothered to keep a gun on him was beyond him. If they fired it in here, it would blow a hole in the side of the jet, and they would all suffer explosive decompression as the air rushed out of the sealed jet. He slowly made his way down the carpeted aisle, passing Archer on the way, who looked a little happier but was apparently hungry again as he went up to one of the guards and pointed a finger at his own mouth.

"Foooooddd. Mooorre." The guards quickly acquiesced, not wanting to face the wrath of the hungry mutant American.

When he had finished his trip to the men's room, Rockson returned to the open passenger section. He was curious about the effects of weightlessness. Under the watchful eyes of the guards, he released himself from the magnetic shoes and leaped up into the air, tucking his legs in under him. He went into a spring that accelerated faster and faster the more he pulled into a tighter circle. His years of physical training and his martial arts abilities made him quickly understand how to move in zero gravity. The Doomsday Warrior took off like an acrobat, soaring around the interior of the jet like some airborne porpoise. Even the guards were impressed, lowering their rifles as they watched the gymnastic performance.

It felt wonderful, Rock thought—like being a child in a dream when one could fly by merely flapping one's arms. He pushed his body to the limits, trying every angle, every torque of hips and arms that he could think of. He glanced down suddenly at the guards and realized that he could easily take them out. A quick push off the top steel-ribbed ceiling and he would be down upon them like a wolf among the chickens. But he wanted to meet Vassily. Who knew where such an encounter would lead?

After about fifteen minutes of weightless gymnastics, Rockson returned to his seat. Both guards smiled at him. They couldn't help but respect the man—his abilities were almost superhuman. They looked at him with strangely friendly eyes. Rock returned the gesture. It was not the common Red troops who were his enemy—even if he did have to kill them when the occasion arose. No, it was the leadership. It had always been—since the dawn of time. Those few, power-mad men who had to rise to the top and let their primitive, sadistic impulses become the rules of life. It was governments that had caused all of man's problems. Wizened old men who sent the young out to die while they stayed at home making pronouncement after pronouncement on the need to kill, to conquer, to destroy. Maybe the world would have been better off if man had never evolved civilization; if man had stayed in the trees, in small clusters. Hadn't the industrial world given humanity myriad ways to die, culminating in the atomic bomb which had turned the blue and green paradise of earth into a living hell? What was it a great philosopher had once said—"Power corrupts—absolute power corrupts absolutely." Rockson suddenly wished that every government official on earth would suddenly disappear—and just the people would be left—the workers, the farmers. They had no wish to destroy one another. Just to live and let live.

The Doomsday Warrior sat back in his seat and

stared out the window. Far below, earth could be seen—its oceans and continents, like a child's jigsaw puzzle, fitting perfectly together. The planet seemed so beautiful, fragile from way up here. The devastation that had been done disappeared at such a height. The Doomsday Warrior felt a surge of tenderness toward his planet. It seemed so small, so vulnerable from twenty-eight miles up. A living, breathing thing that wished only to heal its wounds and create life once again.

Rockson sat back in his seat and remembered what the "Glowers" had taught him—how they had taken him on a mind excursion into the energy currents of the earth. He closed his eyes and sank deep into the meditative state that the strange race had taught him. It took time without the Glowers' help, but after about ten minutes he felt his consciousness begin to rise up and drift free of the physicality that was Ted Rockson. Pure energy, he drifted through the molecular structure of the jet and soared down through the atmosphere. He could feel the cosmic rays shooting down from space, the gravitational pull of the planet like a billion arms grabbing, pulling all solid objects into itself. He flew like a shooting star across the vast cleansing oceans, feeling their tidal swells, the undulations of the waves as they traveled from continent to continent. He dropped lower onto the countries that had once been Europe and saw the people in all their misery—ragged and ill-nourished—hopelessness etched in their eyes as all that they had was consumed by Russian state. He felt their hearts bursting with pain, their children dying. He dropped lower and lower onto the planet and felt it, the soil, the rocks moving just beneath the surface, taking the radioactive poisons deeper down into its burning core trying to neutralize them. In spite of the charnel ground that the war had created, the planet forgave and tried to return to its pure state, tried to purify the soil and the streams in an attempt to recreate itself in the image of a century before.

The Doomsday Warrior saw the thousands of villages, the people reduced to primeval state of savagery—the Russian military fortresses never more than one hundred miles apart with their hordes of food and purified water. He felt that his heart was about to burst—so much pain and suffering. It was beyond the ability of a man to change—so much, so much destruction. And yet in the midst of his anguish, Rock heard the singing voices of the Glowers as if from a million miles away. Encouraging him, pushing him on, sending out their own power and mental strength to give him the will to accept it all.

"Yes, Rockson, yes. You must see it all." He heard their voices in his brain in rippling harmony. Like a memory flying on the winds of the world. "See it—don't turn away. This is the earth as it is. You must understand it all. For you are the man whose destiny it is to change things." Their spirit filled him. And somehow in the midst of his visions of death and de-evolution came a new feeling. The spirit of the heart of man. It never stopped trying to survive. It glowed like a diamond, like the very core of the sun taking what is was given and trying to make it better. This was why it was all worth it. The soul of man itself. The mind, the greed—that was the poison. But the soul, the eternal essence of the human creature — this was the indestructible thing — more brilliant than the exploding supernovas that he could sense far above him, deeper then the oceans. He felt the purity, the nobleness of humanity, and it filled him with a glowing fire that he had never known.

Renewed, Rockson let himself drift back up to the skies, borne aloft by the winds, the heat rising from the sunbaked plains. Like an invisible balloon he floated back up into the thin reaches of the atmosphere. Ahead he saw the Russian jet piercing the dark heavens and somehow, without even knowing the power that enabled him to leap among the very molecules of space, he made his way back through the metal fibers of the craft. He saw his body seated, eyes closed, and entered back into it. Slowly his lids opened and he was back in himself. He felt his body again, and the weight of it took a few seconds to get used to — after the absolute freedom of the mind excursion.

Rock heard a sound at his side and turned. Archer was looking over at him with immense dark eyes beneath jet-black eyebrows. The huge man pointed to his mouth.

"Ungry," he said, "Archer ungry." Rockson let out a laugh that brought the guards to their feet. Life was ugly and it was beautiful. But it was also a joke. A humor beyond understanding.

Chapter Eleven

Rock was surprised that there were no curtains on the windows of the twenty-foot-long sedan that carried them from the airport. He and Archer stared out the windows in fascination as they zoomed along a superhighway filled with traffic toward the Emerald City-like vista before them. Never had he imagined Moscow would look like this: two hundred-story skyscrapers with rapier tops, the sun glinting off the spires which seemed to pierce the low strontium-tinged clouds. But as they drew closer the vision tarnished. Instead of glitter he saw many of the windows of the huge buildings were broken, some of the towers partly in ruins. He noted rust marks down the sides of the smaller stone structures. The stench in the air began to rise — garbage and raw sewage flowing into the Volga River's turbulent waters. The highway ran along the edge of the mighty river, passing groups of sullen workers carrying loads of firewood and produce on towering baskets balanced precariously on their heads. Then he gasped as did Archer. All along one section of the riverbank were crucifixes. Nailed on them were nearly naked men and women, most motionless and slumped forward, their hands and feet nailed tightly into the blood-soaked wood. Hundreds of them, with but a few still alive enough to gaze up at the passing car with unfathomable pain in their foggy eyes.

"Who are they?" Rockson asked one of the guards seated across from him, holding a pistol at the Doomsday Warrior's chest.

The guard leered. "Dissidents — you know, social revisionists, artists, hooligans, gypsies." He glanced out the window at the spread-eagled corpses. "No Americans today. That's unusual — for often the women brought from your country for breeding revolt and kill their masters. Then they are — well. There are none now, for this is a special occasion. You are the premier's special guest. You and your foul friend — and there will be no executions of American women until after you leave. Maybe never, I've heard rumors, if negotiations — but you will see, Ted Rockson. You will see."

"Bastards!" Rock muttered under his breath.

Several miles off Rockson noticed a large dome rising from the flat land around it.

"What's that?" he asked, pointing at the futuristic structure.

"Classified," the guard answered curtly. Then he added with a smirk, "It's why we beat you Americans a hundred years ago. Our technology was more powerful than yours." Rockson filed the information in his brain. He would have to try and find out more about the mysterious complex.

They drove through the crowded streets of Moscow at high speed, forcing pedestrians to leap out of the way of the speeding sleek black limo, red flags on the hood snapping crisply in the wind. Then they entered Red Square, filled with throngs of Russian sightseers. Rock gazed with fascination at the capital of the Soviet Empire: the high walls of the Kremlin, St. Basil's Church with its bizarre, domed towers—a museum, no longer a church—and the tombs of Lenin and Drabkin, the premier who had ordered the strike on America, surrounded by elite color guard with rifles, frozen at attention as still as the dead.

They drove through an ornate iron gate at the Kremlin's back wall and were quickly ushered inside, guards surrounding them, down a plush, spotless red carpet. The air was frigid, air-conditioned—not that it was hot outside—but for the smell that permeated everywhere in Moscow from the garbage-filled Volga.

"The premier will see you shortly," said a white-tuxedoed black man who came up to them, moving gracefully across the vast marbled entrance room. His ebony intelligent face immediately struck Rockson.

"I am Ruwanda Rahallah, the premier's aide and advisor. I welcome you to the Kremlin on his behalf. I trust you have been well treated since you were informed of the meeting."

"Very," Rock answered as Archer nodded, looking around for possible bowls of food. The two freefighters followed the elegantly dressed black man through a series of immense chandeliered rooms filled with wall murals of the revolution. Finally they came to a small book-lined room.

"The premier's study," Rahallah said softly. "Do make yourself comfortable, gentlemen. Perhaps some wine? Chateau Neuf de Pâpe '78—that's *1978*, gentlemen. Care to try some?"

Rockson nodded and they were poured generous glasses of an exquisitely fine wine over a century old. Archer gulped his down to the obvious distaste of the cultured Rahallah.

"A wine beyond price," Rahallah said, gently admonishing his charges, "must be savored, tasted—not gulped."

The premier walked in from a side door. He was a frail-looking man with age spots covering his deeply lined face. He moved a bit shakily but his eyes were as clear and bright as a summer sun. He moved slowly toward Rockson and shook his hand with a soft grip.

"No formalities here, Mr. Rockson, we are—equals. I trust you understand the importance of this meeting for your people. Peace Mr. Rockson—peace." They stared at one another for several moments, trying to take a measure of the other. Then Premier Vassily sat down behind a dark, ancient wooden desk.

"Now Mr. Rockson—and Mr—er—"

"Archer is his name," Rock said with a thin smile, wondering what the premier would make of the huge mute who kept looking around the study as if expecting a woods' animal to pop out from one of the thousands of dusty books that surrounded them.

"Yes — Mr. Archer — I am sorry for the inconveniences my nephew, the well meaning but inept president of — "

"President of *nothing* — " Rock said sharply.

"Of course, of course — Mr. Rockson. That will be negotiated too. His status in *your* land. But these peace talks between us — never forget we are doing this in order to save lives. To save the environment further damage, to — "

"To insure that you will have enough troops you can pull out of the struggle in America to fight your losing battles elsewhere," Rock cut in, determined not to play games with the powerful leader.

"No, no," Vassily said, raising his tired voice, "not at all. I am a man of peace, interested only in sparing our planet and its people any more suffering. But to be a man of peace in such difficult times — I am willing to make some generous concessions." He sat back in his thick leather upholstered armchair and smiled. "But we must not rush — you are no doubt tired from your long journey. There is time enough for our talks. You will be shown all the hospitality afforded the most honored of foreign visitors. Until tomorrow gentlemen." The premier of the all the world bowed slightly toward Rock and then Archer, who smiled through cavity-mottled teeth and returned the gesture, leaning all the way forward in his chair.

They spent the night in palatial rooms — with

119

bars on the windows. A feast of exotic foods was brought to their quarters by a virtual army of waiters, each with a different steaming meal on a silver platter. After they had eaten their fill and were preparing to sleep—in oversized canopy beds that must have dated back to Czarist Russia—the door opened and four young women marched past the elite guards in the hall and toward the two free-fighters. The Americans stared at the bevy of beauties with wide eyes. Each was dressed in shimmering gossamer gowns that revealed all their charms—and there was plenty to reveal.

"We are here—for your pleasure," one of them, a brunette with hair falling to her waist and deep brown eyes as moist as a doe's, said. The girls, none older than twenty, looked at the two freefighters—Rockson with his chiseled rugged features and body of tanned sculpted muscle, and Archer, seven feet of hairy steel hard flesh, and then back at one another and giggled, putting their hands over their red lips. Their firm upturned breasts jiggled as they laughed. Rock and Archer looked at one another as well, and then the Doomsday Warrior shrugged his shoulders.

"Why not," he said with a sly smile. He had been so near death in the last few days, his body still ached with the welts and healing wounds that had been inflicted on him in the torture room. A woman's softness and perfumed limbs would give him life. A man needs a woman as the lungs need air, the stomach food. He was sure Kim would understand—if not, well, she would never know. He had been through too much in this life to turn down pleasure when it was offered. He took on what life threw at him — whether it was death or love.

Archer's face was aglow with the nervous blushing enthusiasm of a boy both frightened and wildly aroused by the sight of a willing woman. He had had but one encounter with the female sex in his life — in the backwoods of mid-America — with a somewhat overweight mountain woman whose husband had died. She had been quite eager and ready to show the huge Archer the ropes. Though confused and a little shy, he had enjoyed it up to a point. But then she had been on the far side of the spectrum of beauty, compared to these lovely ethereal creatures whose fragrant flesh lived only for pleasure.

Rock picked his choice: the brunette who lowered her eyes shyly as he looked at her. She walked quickly over to him and pressed her full breasts against his steel-hard chest. The other three took Archer, who looked bewildered, by the arms and led him off into an adjoining bedroom.

"You are the Rockson," the brunette said, dragging the Doomsday Warrior to the bed. "I have heard much about you even here in Russia. You are reknowned for being both a fighter and lover."

"Make love not war," Rock said grinning, remembering the phrase he had picked up from ancient American newsreels. "But you know so much about me — what of you? What's your name?"

"Svetlanya," the brunette said, rubbing her hands along Rockson's strong chest. "I live only for love. But only with the most powerful and fa-

mous men—kings, rulers—and men like you,
Rockson. Men who are men. And something tells
me you are special." She nuzzled her soft lips
against his neck, moving her lithe full body on top
of his.

"I try," he said grabbing hold of her with his
powerful arms. She moaned and he could smell
the sweet perfume of her aroused sex. She slowly
undid her nearly invisible peignoir and kneeled before him, showing the American the fruits of her
body. She was beautiful—with pointed pink nip-
ples that begged to be kissed and fondled. Her
breasts were firm as ripe melons, swelling out for
his touch. Between her white thighs, a mound of
soft hair that she pushed against his thigh, her
mouth opening in the mindless throes of desire.

Slowly she undressed him, letting out little sighs
of desire as she uncovered his flesh. She lay beside
him, stroking the firm body as her hand moved
slowly downward. She gripped his aroused manhood and a shiver coursed through her body.

"Oh—you are so—so *much* of a man." The
touch of his organ seemed to drive her into a
frenzy. She slid down his now unclothed flesh and
took the rock-hard staff into her ruby lips. Rock
lay back, letting his mind give up all the death he
had seen, the plans he was formulating for action,
and drifted into the pure pleasure of her motions.
She moved up and down on the spear of flesh, letting it go deep into her moist throat, writhing
against him in shivers of uncontrollable passion.
At last he pulled her up until she was alongside
him and rolled on top of the courtesan of ultimate

122

pleasure. He kneaded her firm breasts, squeezing them hard beneath his veined hands. His fingers found her wet treasures below, and he stroked between the swelled lips of her sex. She groaned again, closing her eyes as Rockson spread her firm thighs. He poised above her for a moment and plunged his manhood into the waiting entrance. She squirmed like a creature on fire, wrapping her legs around his broad back as he entered deep into her burning center. He took her with powerful strokes, sensing that she liked to feel the full power of a man. Her eyes closed as she swung her head back and forth beneath his driving motions, in a state of the purest ecstasy.

In the other room the three women who had gone with Archer were wild with excitement. As they had undressed him for his bath, revealed before their wide eyes was the largest male organ they had ever seen. They exclaimed over it, a little frightened of such a tool but eager to sample its abilities. Archer let them do the work. It was clear they knew more about the arts of lovemaking than he. But he was eager to learn. First one, then the other mounted his stiff staff, hardly able at first to get it into them. But once fully inside they rode the steel-hard spear with mad delight as the others rained kisses and caresses on the freefighter's bear-sized physique. They undulated through the long night, taking turns with the apparently untiring Archer, who was more than willing to be used in such pleasurable pursuits.

The next morning Rockson couldn't help but laugh as he saw Archer's tired but happy face. The girls ran past him giggling, out into the corridor. Archer looked at Rock and shook his hand, trying to whistle, although all that came out was a garbled slurping sound. But Rock got the message.

They ate a hearty breakfast, once again brought in by a squadron of servants, and then were brought down to a large council chamber with Russian flags covering the walls. They were seated at a long conference table that stretched nearly fifty feet down the center of the hall. Soon they were joined by the slow-moving Vassily and nearly ten of his political staff.

The negotiations around the polished table lasted nearly all day as Rock and the Reds haggled over every point of a possible treaty. Food and beverages were brought in every few minutes with a wide selection for every possible taste. Rockson was amazed at how Rahallah was always whispering into the frail Vassily's ear. In America he had never seen even one black Russian soldier, let alone officer. Yet here, a black man had input into the highest levels of power. Rock had no intention of carrying out the provisions of the slowly negotiated treaty—besides he was not an elected representative of the new American government anyway. Something the Russians could not understand. To them Rockson was a man of power—his words would be heeded by the freefighters. The Doomsday Warrior was biding his time. He had already developed a plan of sorts, but the moment was not yet right to strike. Better that the Russians believe he was here to make peace. Then their guard would drop.

Any doubts Premier Vassily had that Rockson was not sincere disappeared over the next three days of intense argumentation. The famed resistance fighter did his best to wring the most favorable possible terms—short of removal of all Russian forces from the United States. The agreement that they at last worked out pulled the Reds much further than they had wanted to go.

Vassily looked through the final draft of the peace treaty. The premier had given away more than he wanted to get the peace. But he needed to divert his forces to the battles in China and India, both overrun and cut off from Russia by the Muabir, the Flame of Allah and his fanatical legions of horsemen. Rockson carefully read each provision before initialing them.

1) The Soviet Union will arrest and put on trial Colonel Killov, director of KGB forces, for crimes against humanity and the ecology.

2) The U.S.S.A. will elect a president who will replace General Zhabnov who will become vice president but will retain his role as commander-in-chief of all armed forces. Foreign policy shall remain the domain of the Russian command.

3) The U.S.S.R. will not use atomic or chemical weapons anywhere in the world. Biological weapons that attack only humans, not plant or animal life, and that are of *short* duration will be allowed.

4) Internal affairs of the U.S.S.A. will be governed by an American police force, although the Russian military presence will remain. The crowning point of achievement for Vassily and for which he had given up much was—5) The freefighters

will turn over the technology for the black-beam weapons to the Soviet Union. These could be used by Vassily when all other negotiations had failed to fight insurrections anywhere but not to be used in the U.S.S.A.

6) All food shipments to the Soviet Union will be increased five percent a year until the present yearly figure was doubled. Otherwise the entire agreement is cancelled.

7) American pacification teams will visit sections of the Soviet fortresses in America and make them understand that the treaty prohibits revolt or attacks on Soviet staff or technicians.

8) The freefighters will use their skills to have Rockson help negotiate a treaty with the Muabir for the cessation of hostilities along Russia's southern border.

Rock and Vassily shook hands and the eight provisions of the treaty were initialed by each man. Vassily stood up on wobbly legs and gave Rockson a weak bear hug, then kissed him on both cheeks.

Rahallah and the other advisors present applauded loudly.

"Peace, peace," they shouted as Vassily beamed broadly. At last, thought Rahallah, perhaps Africa will be next.

Rockson was handed one final piece of paper by Vassily.

"What's this?" he asked warily.

"A mere formality," the premier said. "A part of the treaty that will not be promulgated in the U.S.S.A. And it will remain in my vault here in the Kremlin. That is the only copy. You must sign it in order for the rest of the treaty to be in force." Rockson was hardly surprised when he read the addition.

9) In the event of the American partner to this agreement failing to meet their obligations, then the Supreme Soviet State reserves the right to carry out the following: Any large-scale insurrection of the American people will result in a massive nuclear missile ICBM strike at their rebel staging areas—particularly the Rocky Mountains.

"You expect me to sign this?" Rock asked with bitterness.

Vassily pursed his age-cracked lips. "I just want you to see the obvious. You needn't worry about your American friends seeing Article Nine. For your benefit it will not be made public. I want you to know that we will back up the provisions of this treaty with overwhelming might."

"You don't even have ICBMs anymore," Rock said, digging for information.

"Oh, but we do," Vassily said, his eyes tightening. "There are still many functioning silos deep underground in the Caucasus Mountains."

"But that would mean more radioactivity—not just for America—but entire world. The ecology is already—"

"I said *maybe*, Rockson. But should you disobey the provisions of the treaty which I have bent backward to offer the best possible terms out of my desire for peace—then I wish you to understand that our great Satellite and Missile Command Complex, right here on the outskirts

127

of Moscow, will direct a total counterblow against your rebel fighters. And this time it will be the end. Do you hear me, Rockson. I don't wish to further damage our planet but the world must hold together, with one supreme capital—Moscow."

"Yes, I see," Rock said softly, staring at the man he had thought was at a higher level than the other Reds. But Vassily, despite all his learning and pretensions of wanting peace, was part of the pack: power mad, autocratic, and ruthless.

"Hell," he said angrily, as he reached over and scribbled his signature. The treaty would bring *time*—precious time until Rock could find a way out of these walls—and destroy the enemy's very heart: the control center. It had to be the towering dome that he had seen on the way in from the airport.

That night there was an enormous Russian-style banquet with whole stuffed roast pig, baked oxen, caviar, and tables of delectable fruits and vegetables and gourmet treats such as hummingbird tongue pie and salmon paté. Rock and Archer ate their fill with the big mute gobbling up everything in sight as Vassily sat in his wheelchair watching approvingly. They watched a show of belly dancers who gyrated to the accompaniment of a mazooka-balalaika band. Then elite Red Army dancers came out and did some fast-stepping Russian kicks and leaps. They drank as they danced until they fell to the floor unable to stand, to roars of boisterous laughter from the assembled officers and dignitaries who threw their glasses to the floors.

The festivities didn't end until nearly three in the morning. But at last the vast party room was emptied, and Afghani orderlies came in to sweep up the shards of glass that littered the marbled floor.

Chapter Twelve

"It's time, buddy," Rock said, tapping Archer on the shoulder. The big freefighter slowly awoke, looking up with a startled expression at Rockson. "We're going to, as they used to say, break out of this joint." Archer didn't quite understand the expression, but he got the intent of Rock's meaning. He rose and quickly dressed himself in his American clothes: bearskin coat and immense khaki pants. At last he could wear his real clothes again—not the Russian tailored suit they had given him.

The two freefighters made their way quietly to a third room into which Rock knew Archer's crossbow had been put. The door was locked, but several swift kicks from the Doomsday Warrior ripped the lock apart and the thick oak door swung open. They made their way into the darkened suite cautiously but quickly saw that there were no guards present. Rock's gamble that the Russians would grow lax with security, believing that the freefighter had changed his tune, had worked. They found the crossbow, sealed inside a thick plexiglass case, seemingly impenetrable. Rock hefted a metal table lamp and slammed it against the transparent case, but the heavy object bounced off. The case was strong, probably an alloy of some type. He inspected the plexiglass container closely as Archer pressed his face against it, longing to be reunited with his weapon—the closest thing to a security blanket that the fearless seven-foot warrior had. Rock examined every inch of the case looking for a weakness—and found it. Every seam of the plexiglass was sealed and faultless. That gave the Doomsday Warrior an idea. He went over to the large silver samovar filled with steaming water and carried it over to the case. They smashed the wood table beneath and placed the boiling water of the Russian tea-making device beneath it. Rock turned the steam to high and waited. In just minutes the impenetrable case exploded with a loud pop—burst open by air pressure from inside heated by the steam.

Archer sighed as he inspected his tools of the trade, then grunted approval and slapped Rock on the shoulder. They walked to the window—no bars for they were hundreds of feet up—far above the luminous trails of the ground traffic zipping along the wet pavement below them on Dzerjinski Plaza. Rock surveyed the area outside the window. The shutters opened out. A man, if he wanted to, could commit suicide—just stand on the sill and kiss this old life good-bye. It would take forever to reach the pavement and crush some comrade's precious car. For a moment he considered making some sort of glider, remembering flying down off Ice Mountain near Century City in a jury-rigged device with glider wings (See Book #1.) But one glance at Archer's heavy frame convinced him that the giant would not fare well in such an attempt.

There: A ledge. He saw decorative series of faces! Lenin, Bulganin, Stalin, Krushchev, Brezhnev, Titov, and Drushkin—completely girthing the building with their five-foot-high granite features. The only problem was the sculptures started nearly forty feet away, and there was no ledge to crawl along to reach them and the window set between them that would, Rock hoped, lead to rooms unguarded by Imperial Kremlin troops.

"Archer, do you think you could make a shot, I mean a *very good* shot with one of your steel arrows with a line attached to it—and jam the arrow into that gargoyle over there?"

Archer looked over and grunted. He took an arrow from his quiver and handed it to Rockson who attached a thick electrical extension cord to the back—Made In USA it said on it. He pulled on it with all his strength and the cord held. Archer fitted the arrow into the firing slot on the crossbow and fired. His aim was true as chips of gargoyle chest fell and sailed into the blustery wind. Archer watched incredulously as Rock stood on the sill and hauled himself up across the rope. Rockson reached the row of concrete faces and then motioned for Archer to make the journey. The giant's face fell as he looked first at Rockson and then down to the street below. With an audible gulp he slung the bow over his shoulder and, praying silently to whatever gods the strange woodsman believed in, he started across. The cord stretched and quivered violently as if protesting the weight on it — but it held. Archer was surprisingly agile for a man his size and immensely strong. If nothing else, his fear of dropping propelled him quickly across the line.

The two freefighters edged along the two-foot-wide ledge beneath the gargoyles, hugging the wall as they moved one careful step at a time. Rock reached a large window and peered quickly inside — empty. He tried it and it opened easily. No one expected entry from the outside — not at this height. He and Archer jumped in and made their way in the darkness to the door. Rockson pulled it and it opened. He put his ear to the crack — nothing.

Moving like cats, they made their way down the carpeted hall heading toward the elevators. Suddenly Rock heard Russian voices — damn — guards in front of the elevator. He should have known. He and Archer came rushing around the corner and at the three guards like bats out of hell. The men barely had time to look up before they were pummeled beneath the fists of the Americans. Rock and Archer dragged the three Reds into a utility closet, and Rockson changed clothes with one, putting the brown Kremlin Guard uniform over his own clothes. It was a tight fit but it would have to do.

Great—now they were free inside the towering building—just untold stories and guards everywhere to get through. "If you don't mind I'm going to bind you," Rock said, taking some cord from a shelf. Archer did mind. A life of being attacked by creatures and Reds from every quarter didn't make him too happy about having his mobility stopped. But for Rockson he would do it. The Doomsday Warrior made the knot loose. Archer could free himself in a second.

They took the elevator down to the main floor and walked past a group of half asleep guards who looked up startled to see the giant. "Taking this foul creature for a bath," Rock muttered in Russian, keeping his cap low over his face. "The premier can't stand the stench." The guards laughed loudly and let them pass. Later they would pay with their lives. Rockson knew they'd have a hard time making it out the front gate where the troops would be much more alert. He saw a stairway exit marked "basement" and they headed down. After marching around the immense storage and boiler rooms they found three steel dumpsters filled with garbage and reluctantly hid themselves under the rotting refuse.

Fortunately they didn't have to wait long. Within an hour huge trucks drove down a ramp and loaded the garbage containers onto their backs. The trucks drove out through the Kremlin walls and down the now nearly deserted highway toward the dump at the outskirts of Moscow. When their truck slowed for a turn, the two freefighters leaped out. They were free in the heart of the Russian capital.

Rock wanted to find the Satellite and Missile Control Center. He had an idea born of desperation and dependent on luck and surprise. Balls were the key to the whole thing. The destruction of the complex would cripple the Red empire's ability to launch any ICBM strikes against America. If it could be taken out—destroyed beyond repair—he doubted the Reds had the technical know-how to put humpty-dumpty together again. But the plan was easier said than done.

They made it through twisting streets to the edge of a park that sat in the center of Moscow, complete with gardens and winding paths. But they had barely entered the grassy terrain when they were spotted by a horde of submachine gun-toting MKVD special forces in blue berets who were double-timing it toward them. There were times when retreat was the better part of valor. They had gone through too much in their escape, and Rock knew they wouldn't get a second chance.

They sped back out of the park and into the narrow dark streets that wound through the metropolis. In this section of the city most of the buildings were run-down, crumbling—obviously homes for the less fortunate of the Russian workers. They were only blocks ahead of the pursuing troops who screamed out at one another as they searched every doorway. Walkie-talkies crackled, and Rockson knew that within minutes the entire area would be saturated with Reds. They turned a dark corner and found themselves in a dead end, facing a twenty-foot-high brick wall. The troops closed in.

Suddenly they heard a sound just behind them. A manhole grate opened and a voice said, "Pssst!" They rushed over ready to battle and saw a small man dressed in a black robe emerge from the hole. His hair was white as snow and with his black wrap-around sunglasses he made quite a sight.

"In here friends," he said in heavily accented English. They had no choice. Reds were just around the corner. Rock decided to trust the man and slid down the opening. Archer had a hard time getting in but at last squeezed through, pulling down the cover just as tramping Red feet rushed overhead. Their benefactor motioned for them to follow him. He pulled out a pencil flashlight and though dim, they were able to make their way through the six-foot-wide sewer tunnel. They walked for nearly half an hour. Then the tunnel suddenly widened and they stepped into a large open cavern. Rockson gasped. It was a subway station, old and dusty. A large group of similarly clad smallish men with the same white hair stood waiting. Rock stayed Archer's hands as he whipped up his crossbow.

"Hold it Archer—these are friends." Rock hoped he was right. The black-robed men held weapons in their hands that were oddly shaped, almost like musical instruments from what he could make out in the dim light of the flickering electric chandeliers above. Rock stepped up to them and looked the group over.

"You speak English?" he asked.

"Oh very good English," the tallest of the lot

said, moving forward until he stood just a foot away. "I be Yuri Goodman Chekhov and this," he continued, sweeping his hand over the men behind him, "be my proud people. The dissidents, they call us. We live down here—not too bright, and *cool*. These be the old subway system of this big bad city. We like America," he said animatedly. "You know any jazz musicians in your country? They still play in nightclubs over there? Do you like Coltrane? Do you have a sax?" The questions flowed one after another as the other dissidents looked on with interest.

Rock stared at the man incredulously, not quite knowing what to say. "Are you all musicians? I see you're holding a clarinet."

"Oh," Yuri Goodman said with a smile, "this not regular clarinet. This be weapon, too—sonic boom-boom. Understand?"

Rock stared blank-faced. "Here I show you." Goodman laughed. He looked around the dilapidated subway station until he saw a quick movement at one end. "There we go—mouski—now we show you American jazz friends how we play instruments." He pointed his brass clarinet toward the mouse and played a sweet extremely high note. The mouse froze, then shivered and dropped dead. Yuri Goodman removed the reed from his mouth. "See—do same thing to Red troops. Like gun— only more fun to shoot. Dig us, American jazz friends, where are your instruments? We could have groovy jam sessions. Is that not what you do all time in America—sit in jazz clubs and play with black friends and all races?" Rock looked on, his jaw hanging open. "We dig American jazz. We all right dissidents."

"Right," they yelled in harmony. "We dig jazz."

"Why you not sit down with us in club called Fat Black Pusscat and we play swinging stuff by Mingus and Ellington? If you don't have instruments — we loan. What you American hipsters play? Vibes? An axe?"

Rock tried to explain that he was an American soldier, but Yuri Goodman only said, "You have big band sound — do jitterbug and with your sweetie you dance in PX?" This was getting them *nowhere*.

They were led to a small shack at one end of the station that could barely be called a structure, so rotting were its walls and ceiling. Rock and Archer sat down and rested. The other dissidents sat down around them at tables with candles in the center of each in the dark make-believe American style coffee shop of the mid-1960s. How in God's name they had gotten photographs of such places or picked up all the lingo they used was beyond Rockson's comprehension. He looked around: The subway station was really more of a terminal. High marbled walls with murals beautifully embedded in them of proud Russian farmers in their bright red tractors, of workers holding wrenches as they worked inside huge factories. Drawings in red and blue and orange and black square tiles. Rock had to admire their beauty — he had never been a great fan of Socialist Realism art, but these had a certain primitive nobility.

The dissidents had set up their permanent home

within the terminal with sleeping bags and hammocks hung from ancient rusting lamps and pipes that ran along the walls and ceilings which rose nearly sixty feet above the platforms. Tracks on each side of the terminal disappeared far off into the darkness. On one side sat a ten-car-long Russian subway obviously not used for nearly a century—its wheels rusted down into red metal dust, its cars filled with decades of dirt and spiderwebs.

"How the hell did this place get going?" Rock asked Yuri who sat across from him, his clarinet resting across his knees.

"Years ago, the subways ran bopping through these groove tubes. But a big boom-boom tube, one of yours, wipe out the north section. Reds let place rot, like burgers and fries. We blew into the scene and just crashed here. Now—it's our permanent digs. You dig?"

"I see," Rock said, sipping espresso that was handed to him by a black-leotarded female dissident waitress who slinked away, snapping her fingers.

"So, what's your scene?" Yuri Goodman asked curiously. "I mean, what kind of jive you into—really?"

Rock gulped down the delicious bitter brew and decided to trust the man. He had nothing to lose, and the dissidents appeared to hate the Reds as much as any freefighter.

"You know the domed Satellite and Missile Control Center?" the Doomsday Warrior asked.

"Of course," Yuri said, sipping his own steaming cup of expresso.

140

"I want to blow it up. Can you help us American jazz men play that tune?"

"Blow up the big egg? Why not shoot down Red jazz haters with our clarinets and tubas? Why destroy pretty egg building?"

Rock explained just what the dome meant as Yuri listened intently.

"That be different story, crazy swinger. If it can save the world for Glenn Miller dances and swinging times on crazy blue nights — then we try. What you need?"

"Explosives — I don't suppose you have any?"

"Explosives — no. Why need? Oh, I see what you mean — boom-boom stuff."

"Yes, boom-boom stuff," Rock said excited. "Do you know where we can get some?"

"We got a whole room full. Used to build tunnel for new line. Before mega-mothers hit. Got lots of boom-boom. Enough to turn egg into red-hot omelette."

Chapter Thirteen

Archer never liked never being underground. He was a man of the open fields, the mountains. Even in Century City, Archer had, despite its airy plazas and wide underground passageways, felt claustrophobic. Here in the ancient Moscow subways he felt doubly uncomfortable. Once outside the large terminal the ceilings were oppressively low in sections, and Archer kept bending his seven-foot-plus frame for fear of scraping his head. He took to wearing an ancient WW II Russian Army helmet provided by the dissidents. He walked around, mouthing annoyed grumbles and grunts that no one could understand.

The next morning Archer woke up early, before Rock, and headed off down the tunnel in search of the toilet facilities that the dissidents had shown him. He walked through the dark tunnel lit by an occasional flickering light bulb that the jazzmen had strung up every few hundred feet, run by stolen electricity from passing power lines. Somehow he managed to take a wrong turn and headed deeper into the depths, sure that he would stumble upon the tunnel latrine. Within minutes he was completely lost within the labyrinth of the elaborate unused Moscow subway system. He began groaning and rushing this way and that, desperately hoping he would stumble upon the way out. He could take on twenty men at a time but to be lost underground scared the giant half to death. He pulled out the little penlight flashlight the dissidents had given him and Rock, but it was hardly enough to do more than dimly light up a few steps ahead. The immense freefighter was sure that he saw thousands of little green eyes peering at him from out of the impenetrable darkness of the endless tunnel. Rats? Mutated bugs? If they were big enough and would come forward he would tear them apart. But no, they hovered in the distance, watching, waiting as he lost himself deeper within the subterranean world.

At last he came into one of the wider chandeliered stations with several of the lights still working. Here the thousand green eyes disappeared, not wishing to enter the brightness. Archer sat down on a half rotted passenger bench near the center of the station and tried to figure out just what the hell to do next. He saw a shiny object at one end of the seat and reached over. It was a small metal flute, probably one of the dissident's, dropped here by accident. The huge freefighter picked it up and lifted it to his lips. He began playing — mournful, sorrowful notes, a slow anarchistic tune that would have warmed the heart of any Zen master of the late Twentieth Century world. Each poignant note echoed down the multiple tunnels that led out of the terminal.

It didn't like music. It had been scared many times, nearly killed by the dissidents and their screaming musical weapons. It had no name. It was forever. It was simply—it. It especially didn't like this music! But this music could be approached and the player could be eaten! It shifted its huge eight-hundred-pound frame, slurped the last of the old bones it was cracking to suck out the sweet marrow. But why eat stale things when fresh warm musicians could be had?

It was round like a ball with seven arms, seven red eyes, seven legs, and seven stomachs—each growling to be fed. It had been formed long ago out of the radioactive pollutants washed into the Volga's churning waters, coursing through the megalopolis of Moscow. It had eaten an occasional lone boater then, long ago, before the sky changed color, before the river ran red with blood. It had retreated into the subways and the sewers where the water ran a foul green. Now it ate rats and cats and ugly things slimy and quick—and occasionally a dissident if he was foolhardy and was alone and lost. But it was hungry now for fresh meat. It hadn't eaten warm flesh for a long time. But now—now it was time to feed. It came down the tunnel running, not caring if it was heard—for how could anything stop it?

Archer heard the dreadful squishing sounds of

the thing's many feet. He spun around and auto-loaded an arrow into his crossbow, the awesome weapon that never left his side. "Shiiit!" he growled, a word he had heard Rockson utter so many times in tight situations that he had begun to use it, though speech wasn't his strong point. Something was coming at him—and whatever it was he was sure he didn't want to make its acquaintance. He edged backward on the dimly lit platform, pointing the small tight beam of the flashlight into the darkness of the tunnel. It came out of the twisted shadows on running, tearing feet—enormous, full of teeth, moving forward rapidly, its seven clawed arms flailing at the dank air like a windmill.

Archer let loose a hail of arrows, fed quickly into the crossbow by his autofeed. Most of them seemed to bounce off the hard scales of the thing, but two stuck in crevasses between the creature's armor. The hideous mutation let out a scream of pain and retreated back into the edge of the tunnel, but Archer could see the multiple arms pulling out the stuck arrows as it disappeared. The huge freefighter gulped—his arrows could usually make mincemeat of anything—even a snar-lizard but this . . .

It was mad now. Nothing had ever hurt it before. It had never known the meaning of pain. For the first time in its putrid existence it felt rage. It was beyond hunger now—it thirsted for vengeance. It ripped the arrows from its slimy flesh and threw them on the tracks. Its green blood quickly coagulated, the polluted corpuscles forming a wall of putrescence which hardened within seconds. The pink thing must die. But it must be clever — the pointy things hurt it. It knew the tunnels well and rushed to the side through an opening. It would come around on the pink creature from the back. Soon it would eat.

Archer stood in the center of the terminal platform, spinning around, trying to keep an eye on every corner. He sensed that the creature would be back — anything that could pull his razor-tipped hunting arrows out of its flesh was tough. Too tough. If only Rockson was here — he'd have a plan. He would be clever. Archer racked his brain trying to think of a way out, trying to be smart like Rockson. It had to be able to die. What the hell was, this thing anyway? *Think! Think!* Was there any vulnerability exposed in its charge? But he didn't have time for his philosophical musings. Suddenly there was a sound from behind him — the squishing noise.

He turned raising his crossbow — four arrows in the autofire. He had left the rest of his quiver back at the dissident's encampment because he had been working sharpening the tips. Four shots and then the creature appeared at the far end of the narrow subway platform that had once teemed with rushing workers — now home to nothing but spiders and squealing rats who watched the impending battle from their holes. The monstrous slime thing came slowly toward him, its seven eyes burning with the black glow of death. It let out a roar that sounded like a contemptuous laugh, a challenge to the pink thing. Do what you can — for soon you will die. Archer backed down the platform slowly, keeping his eyes fixed directly on the approaching thing.

Suddenly it charged, moving at incredible speed for something so large and foul. The huge freefighter sighted his bow at its face and neck, at least at where he thought they were, because it was such a mass of oozing filth it was hard to tell where any part of it began or ended. He fired one after another of the deadly arrows. But this time the thing was smart. It flailed at the approaching shafts with its many arms knocking them from the air. One caught it just below one of its dripping claws, but it whipped the appendage to the side and the arrow flew out again, hardly able to lodge within the swampy mass. Now what appeared to pass for a smile crossed its immense saliva-coated jaws. It knew the pink thing had run out of weapons. It would savor the meal.

Archer ran backward, not wanting to take his eyes from it. He suddenly had the terrible vision of those teeth and claws ripping into his flesh. It would be ridiculous to die here at the hands of this thing after all he had been through, after all the Russians and beasts of the American wastelands he had defeated. His back foot bumped into something, and he fell over on his side, slamming onto the cold concrete platform with a resounding thud. The thing rushed forward, knowing the time was right. Its dark jaws opened to their full extent as it could taste the prey just seconds away. Archer scrambled furiously on the dirt-coated concrete floor as if trying to swim away from his grisly fate.

His hand made contact with a long fallen pole that had once held a lamp in more civilized days. It was nearly eight-feet long, broken near the tip which was now razor sharp with rusted, pointed edges. The thing launched itself through the air, pushing up with all the strength of its seven legs. Archer whipped the pole around, resting the bottom just under his armpit so it touched the stone floor. The makeshift spear caught the hungry creature dead center, ripping right through its middle. What passed for its heart deep inside was cut to pieces as it hung on the staff feet above Archer, whipping its appendages around furiously.

It felt pain—unbearable pain. It had thought in its dim mind that it was eternal—that as it had no beginning it had no end. But suddenly it knew that it was gone. It could feel its heart tear and then a numbness that spread out from its center to every cell. A cold pain that grew with every second. It snapped its row of bent teeth, trying to reach the pink thing, trying to take it along on its journey into hell, but it couldn't. Then it felt a darkness descending on its senses. A darkness into eternity.

Archer slid out from beneath the dangling putrescence as its thick green blood dribbled down onto him. He rolled quickly to the side, letting go of the iron staff, and the dead creature slammed onto the platform just inches away. He jumped up, searching frantically around for another weapon, and ran a few yards. Then he turned and knew—it was gone. A thin smile crossed his lips. He had won. Rockson would be proud.

Somehow the mute made his way back to the

dissident's encampment. He emerged from the tunnel coated with the thick green blood of the dead creature. The dissidents looked at him curiously as Rockson walked over with a grin on his face.

"You look like you've been doing battle with an artichoke," the Doomsday Warrior said.

Archer nodded furiously. "Artechooke," he said, pumping his hands up and down to simulate the killing action of the spear.

"Jesus, you smell," Rock said, holding his fingers over his nose. The dissidents, too, backed away as the odor was quite unpleasant. Two of them waved for Archer to follow them, and they led him to their makeshift shower, using water siphoned off from a passing water main. Soon the freefighter was clean again, but he knew he would never quite be able to explain just what had gone on deep below the Moscow streets.

The next day—if one could say day here in the unchanging subterranean world—Yuri Goodman brought in a wizened, stooped old man on crutches they called Satchmo, who spoke English better than the others of his clan.

"I learned from record covers—you understand?" he said to Rockson who shook his hand warmly. "What style you into, big boy?" the ancient Jazzman asked. "Bop? Swing? Cool? Progressive?"

Rock stuttered, trying to remember his history tapes back in Century City, not wanting to insult Satchmo. They obviously took their music seriously here.

"Ummm—Dixieland. Always loved it," Rock said.

"The *roots* man! Cat digs the roots of swing," the jazzman said smiling, looking around at the dissidents nearby. They all nodded in approval. "You all right," he added, looking at Rock with increased respect. "I understand you want the explosives?" He wore no sunglasses, and Rock suddenly saw by his unmoving gaze that the man was blind.

"Yes—but how can you show me?"

"I have sort of a built-in radar for these tunnels. When the eyes go, the ears and the senses become sharper. You dig?" Archer and Rock along with a small group of dissidents who held their instruments at the ready in case of trouble, followed the blind Satchmo through the dim tunnels for nearly an hour and hundreds of twists and turns. Rats and other creatures scurried away as the party approached. At last they reached a dusty storeroom filled with stolen goods: everything from golf clubs to banana clips and old Russian rifles, and crate after crate of dynamite.

"Help yourself," Satchmo said. "My generation were pack rats. We gathered our stuff from the city above. Many of us went up into streets during the Revolution of 2013 when we tried to retake Moscow. They all died—only those who stayed in the tunnels and I—for I was blind by then—survived."

Rock went through the crates carefully examining the state of the goods. He found it all in apparently functioning condition, along with fuses and blasting caps. It would do—it would have to.

151

Chapter Fourteen

The best laid plans of mice and dissidents . . .
After they lugged nearly a ton of the explosives
back to the encampment, Rock wanted to test
them just to make sure. With three of the dissidents leading him and Archer they made their way
several miles to an immense linking terminal where
ten sets of tracks met. The space was wide and
high enough for Rockson to see just what the effects of the antiquated dynamite would be. They
set ten sticks in the curved wall of one of the tunnels with a one-minute timer and ran back to
safety. The stuff went off with a thunderous roar,
and when they went back to check, they found
that it had indeed torn out a ten-foot chunk of the
solid rock.

They were just leaving the terminal when they
heard noises behind and ahead of them. Reds — on
one of their infrequent attempts to track down the

homebase of the dissidents. They tore down the tunnel from all directions in search of the creators of the explosion.

Colonel Dzeloski stared down the dark subway tube with his special night-vision glasses. There — there they were about a quarter mile ahead — the swarthy creatures — but there appeared to be two large men with them, one of them nearly twice as tall as the jazzmen. Could it be — he had heard of the escape of the freefighters. It had been a humiliation for the premier. If he could capture them . . . He screamed out orders to his men — an elite squad of MKVD troops — broken into four-fifty man units. "Get them! Forget about the dissidents. I want those two!" Troops coming from a linking tunnel were just a few hundred feet from the fleeing rebels. The colonel screamed out orders through his walkie-talkie. "Flank them! Bring up the flamethrowers." The dissidents saw that they were cut off. Reds were coming at them from both ends of the tunnel. The jazzmen raised their clarinets as Archer and Rock raised their weapons. A slew of arrows and slugs and ear-piercing notes tore into many a Red, but there were just too many of them. The dissidents rushed forward for a better aim, and the flamethrowers went off, turning the three guides into a mass of burning putty. The fallen bodies lit the tunnel with flickering shadows. Now troops were upon the two Americans, filling the tunnel from every side. The colonel instructed the throwers to be extinguished.

"Stun gas load," he commanded the first ten kneeling soldiers. The colonel watched as three more of his men keeled over from the arrows and bullets of the fiercely fighting Americans. "Fire," the Red commander yelled, and ten gas shells shot out down the tunnel. It took only seconds. Rock and Archer felt themselves growing dizzy and then slumped to the ground unconscious. The colonel ran forward and turned the limp bodies over. It was them—his career had just taken a giant step. "Quickly to the surface with these two. Forget the dissidents for today. These are worth all of those white-faced mutants put together. And a medal for every man here. The premier will be serving us hors d'oeuvres from his own hand inside the Kremlin walls by tomorrow night."

When Rockson awoke he was chained to a stone wall in a crude concrete cell with barred windows high above. There was straw on the floor and a metal shield, battered and dented on the far wall. Rock stood up and nearly tumbled to the ground. His legs were still unsteady from the gas attack. How long had he been under? His chains were long enough to allow him to jump up and catch hold of the bottom of the window. He peered out onto an immense arena with stands filled with seats rising as high as the eye could see. Where the hell was he? He dropped down and stumbled over to the small barred window of a thick wooden door at one end of the cell. There were more cells across from him, each with a prisoner.

"Anyone out there?" he yelled across the straw-littered corridor. A familiar voice groaned back.

"Rooockson!" At least Archer was still alive. The Doomsday Warrior pushed against the door with all his strength. Nothing. The thing must be bolted with steel. Suddenly he heard a clanking and a guard came into view. He was bald and quite large, only a few inches shorter than Archer with a face full of scars and thick muscular arms. He wore a thick leather vest and black leather pants and carried a large sword in a scabbard at his side. He looked at Rockson with his one good eye, the other covered by a patch, and spoke through a long jaw that appeared distended, perhaps reset after being broken.

"Against the wall," he shouted to Rockson, "Or I don't bring this food in." Behind him two men pushed a large vat filled with a pungent meat stew. Rock was starving. He must have been out for days. He retreated to the far wall. The guard opened the door and the assistants filled a large bowl and handed it to the Doomsday Warrior.

"Where am I?" he asked, taking the food in his still trembling hands. The guards laughed loudly at the question, quite amused.

"Where are you? In the pits of hell. In the training rooms of the gladiators. You're going to be entertainment for the rich and powerful in just a few days. This is where slaves and troublemakers come to die." He looked Rockson over. "You look strong. You'll put a good show for the crowd before you get cut to ribbons." He started back toward the door, then turned. "Eat well, my American friend—you will need all your strength. Those who wash out on the first day of gladiator training are disposed of." He slammed the wooden door shut and headed across the corridor where the servers opened the door a crack and slipped food into Archer who growled and slammed against the quickly shut wood. They moved on down the rows of cells doling out the stew to each occupant.

So they had decided to send Rock to the gladiator games. He had heard some of the troops talking about the upcoming contests of warriors when he had been the guest of the premier back in the Kremlin. Vassily had obviously decided there was nothing further to be gained in dealing with the freefighters. And Rock could hardly blame him. He had had no intention of honoring the absurd dictates of the treaty, a document that would have sent the U.S. into legalized slavery forever.

An hour later the guard, this time with an escort of equally tough-looking comrades, returned.

"Time for beginner's class." He smiled as he led Rock and Archer from their cells. "I hope you guys are as fierce as you look. The chief gladiator will test your abilities today and decide whether to have you compete in one of the lesser games. The premier is quite interested in seeing your performance. I understand you—annoyed our esteemed leader." He sneered at the word leader. The man had little regard for the power elite of Russia. He was as cynical as they came, having witnessed enough death for a thousand lifetimes. Perhaps he could be useful.

"What's your name?" Rockson asked.

"Funny you should ask," the scar-faced gladiator said. "I don't remember. Been hit in the head too many times. Just call me Keeper—that's what they all call me. I've been in combat for nearly twenty years — and never lost. So don't try anything on me. There are crucifixes outside the arena with the rotting flesh of those who tried to jump me and escape. A most painful death I am told. If you are a good gladiator you will live well for a brief time and die by the sword — not by crucifixion. Believe me — it's the man's way to go."

After that kind of advice Rock and Archer were led to one section of the vast dirt-covered arena where men were practicing with various weapons — sending out chips of bark as they chopped away at tree branches, snapping whips with loud cracks through the cold winter air, learning to punch and kick by immense trainers who kept knocking them to the ground with a single punch of their ham-sized fists. They trained with broadswords, pikes, tridents, sabers, maces, and battle-axes, desperately trying to gain the skills that would give them a fighting chance against the highly trained gladiators they would soon be facing.

"These are the two Americans — Rockson and Archer," the Keeper said to a man who made *him* look scrawny. The gladiator's girth was that of Archer's, his broad arms even thicker. His sharp blue eyes bore into the American pair with disdain.

"The Americans? How am I supposed to train them? It is said Americans are wild, uncontrolled beasts. Feed them to the animals would be better — "

"Orders are to train them in combat," the Keeper snapped back. "For the Centennial spectacle. The big one in net and trident, and the mutant here," he said, pointing to Rock, "in duo-blade. The premier's orders."

The huge trainer sneered. "Duo-blade? That weapon is only for the most skilled. The premier wants to assure this man's death. It takes years to learn duo-blade. So be it." He turned toward the freefighters. "American scum — you will call me Trigrily. I am also known as the Mauler — so don't get any funny ideas. Now," he said with a smile, "we begin the training."

Archer was handed his trident and net. He took it and looked around wondering. But a glance at the sub-toting guards who ringed the lower seats of the stands quickly dissuaded him of the notion. Rock stared at the odd weapon that the Mauler handed him. It had a fist grip in the center from which two weapons extended on each side. One was a two-edged, razor-sharp blade nearly a foot-and-a-half long, on the other end a hooklike attachment that looked like it could rip a man's intestines out. Rock wondered if he could learn this new weapon well enough to make french fries out of his opponents.

There were about seventy-five gladiators in training on the dusty field, and they were all going at it with a vengeance under the careful eyes of their whip-master trainers. There were pygmies riding each other's shoulders, wielding samurai swords that cut the air with a whoosh before decapitating melons. There were short, squat, hairy, almost apelike men who were practicing strangling treelimbs or crushing enormous hollow steel globes with their bare hands. Mutants and strange races of all sorts filled the arena floor, mock fighting one another, even a few Amazonlike green-haired women who slammed their axes into thick logs over and over, sending up clouds of sawdust. All were intent on surviving the ordeal ahead. They had to win their battles to live. A gladiator vanquished, beheaded, would mean a few more days of training, of life, sweet, horrible life for them.

Rockson was taken aside by a fairly stocky fellow who didn't seem unkind. At first the Doomsday Warrior dismissed the man's abilities due to his portliness and jowly face, but he quickly showed himself to be fast, cunning, and an expert with the lethal duo-blade. "You don't have a chance," were the first words he said to Rock. "But I'm going to do my damndest to teach you everything I know anyway. I hold no love for the masters of these games. We are all slaves under the Reds. But make no mistake: As tough as you may be, your opponent will be the strongest man you have ever faced." He showed Rock how to keep the wrist as loose as possible so as to be able to spin the weapon from side to side. "Flexibility is the key to the duo-blade," he said over and over after every move, as if wanting to imprint the words on Rockson's brain. "Once you tighten up, you're dead." He showed the Doomsday Warrior how to feint, parry and thrust, how to catch an opponent's weapon with the hooked end, spin it and then attack with the blade. They practiced together for nearly three hours under the cold silvery Moscow sky that threatened snow that somehow never quite fell.

Suddenly there was a great commotion at one end of the arena. All stopped in their tracks, swords frozen in midair. A princely-looking man garbed in silk tunic and turban with an entourage of several dozen men entered the training area and behind them, walking step by arrogant step was a gargantuan man. He was nearly stark naked, except for a leopard loincloth, and black as ebony. He must have stood nearly eight feet tall and made even Archer appear small. A red-eyed megaman who snarled and spat with jaws of double rows of hooked teeth. The gladiators in training stared in amazement, not just at his size and obvious power but at the third arm he possessed which came from the center of his chest and which was clearly as strong and mobile as the foot-and-a-half thick arms that dangled at his side. He stopped and stared around at the slave fighters, and his mouth widened into a grotesque smile. Then he laughed.

Rock's duo-blade trainer leaned over and whispered, "That's the one they call the Black Menace, especially bred for generations is his kind. See that third arm and those rows of teeth? Watch them carefully. He's been known to reach down in the midst of a fight and rip the head from his opponent with a single snap of his jaws."

"Why should I have to watch them?" Rock asked, a little nervously. "I have no intention of getting near that charming fellow at all."

The trainer stepped back. "Rockson, didn't they tell you? *You* are to fight the Black Menace in a week's time, armed only with the duo-blade. No —

they didn't tell you." He could see by Rock's wide eyes that it was all a rude surprise. "Train well, my friend. I will teach you all that I know. But no one has defeated him—or even come close. They are raised on genetic farms in Africa solely for the Moscow Gladiator Arena. You haven't much of a chance. But you, too, are some sort of mutant, are you not—with your strange mismatched eyes and that streak of white in your black hair. Perhaps you have a chance—you are strong. But practice, Rockson, practice. You have one week. Shall we begin again?"

Rock looked at the giant black man with some trepidation. The Menace caught his glance and stared back. He raised all three arms forward and squeezed his hands tightly shut as if strangling the Doomsday Warrior from a hundred feet away. Then he laughed again and turned. The procession headed off once again, disappearing into the dark doorway of the arena, holding pens.

"Train me well," Rockson said, turning back to the master of the duo-blade. "I'm not ready to die."

Chapter Fifteen

Buglers stood on every parapet surrounding the coliseum, announcing with their clarion calls the start of the Games of Death. Immense Red flags flapped briskly in the fall wind. Far below, the vast dirt-covered arena awaited the blood that would soon soak into its parched soil. The day of the gladiators had arrived. The rulers of the world, the bureaucrats of Moscow, resplendent in their medal-bedecked, razor-pressed uniforms filled the stands of the coliseum, accompanied by their overly made-up mistresses. They greeted one another with the usual platitudes. The elite of the world — the men who ran the Soviet Empire. And as if their bloody domination wasn't enough — now they thirsted for the blood of the arena. Safe in the stands with their flasks and fur coats they bristled with excitement as this was going to be a special day, indeed.

The Moscow Coliseum had been modeled after the ancient Roman arena both in shape and in function: to make death become a performer for jaded eyes. But this arena was even larger than the ancient crumbling piece of antiquity that stood in ruins in Soviet-occupied Rome. Its vast rows of steel seats could hold nearly one hundred thousand people, and today, they would be filled to capacity. Fifty thousand seats reserved for the elite of the elite and fifty thousand of the higher rows for lower level functionaries. All had blood lust in their eyes.

The men who ran the death games knew they had to fulfill their spectators' expectations, otherwise they might well end up themselves taking part in the bloodletting below. The commissar of entertainment, as he was euphemistically called, was Commissar Dubrovnik, a short but muscular man who had worked his way up to the top through backstabbing and double-dealing at every step of the way. He had left a trail of bodies behind him and protected his privileged post, his mansion by the Volga, with narrow eyes and spies planted everywhere. Dubrovnik, as soon as he had reached this pinnacle of success, had studied the ancient Roman games thoroughly, filled with admiration at the myriad ways they had invented for a man to die. And this—this was the biggest event of the year—the celebration of the Russian conquest of the world a century before.

Games were held weekly, but they were often run-of-the-mill overweight gladiators ripping each other apart with unimaginative and hardly graceful thrusts and smashes of their giant swords. But today was different. The Day of the Games—a once a year spectacle that rivaled anything the Romans could have imagined. Dubrovnik had made sure that this would be a festival of blood that none would ever forget. He sat at a glass-enclosed booth high atop the stadium walls, earphones around his head and a microphone pressed against his lips, shouting out orders to his hundreds of underlings who rushed frantically around the immense stadium making sure that everything would proceed smoothly. They knew that mistakes, delays of the game would be dealt with harshly—very harshly.

At last the stands were filled to bursting, and Dubrovnik, over towering ten-foot-high speakers placed every two hundred feet along the surrounding walls, welcomed the fans to the games.

"Welcome to the Day of the Games," he said, speaking slowly in his deep, nationally known voice. For Dubrovnik had made certain that he was the announcer on most of the important games, introducing the gladiators, many of whom were heroes of the Soviet Union—with their own millions of rubles of reward money for having survived so long. Such names as the Red Lancer, whose long, razor-sharp spear had dissected many an adversary; the Netman, whose dazzling net work pulled opponents from their feet so that his short sword could finish them off; Two-Sworded Mikael, whose dazzling blades could whip a man into so much bloody meat before he had time to know what hit him; and of course—the infamous

Black Menace, the toughest of the tough, who to date had over two hundred kills to his name. One of the few blacks allowed the privileges of the elite he was even welcomed to Kremlin parties. Although the generals and bureaucrats kept a nervous distance from this eight-foot warrior of death. All would fight today. And some would die.

"I am proud," Dubrovnik continued, "to start the Games of Death. I promise you all, you will not be disappointed." Then in that famous four word sentence he started the blood sport. "Gladiators prepare to die."

Dubrovnik liked to start the games off slowly, gradually building the intensity, the danger, until it peaked in the final fight of the big name gladiatores. He had learned how to tease and play with the crowd's emotions, make them want more and more blood and death, until after hours of murder and decapitation they would go home satisfied, excited, and take out their own violence on their mistresses and wives.

Gates opened at each end of the nearly five hundred foot in diameter circular area floor, and young women emerged, terrified, barely clothed, pushed out unwillingly by the probing tips of guards' spears. Nearly fifty of them—slaves taken from various of the empire's vassal nations—all young and pretty. They had already been used by those who desired them and now were discarded to meet their fate in a way more horrible than any could imagine. They gathered together in the center of the arena to the roaring jeers of the bloodthirsty crowd. They stared around with wide panic-stricken eyes, begging for mercy from an audience that had not one drop of mercy to give. Suddenly a large gate at the far end of the arena grounds opened. Deep guttural roars emerged from the darkness. Within seconds they emerged—lions, tigers, leopards, all snarling, angry at their captivity, starved for days and ready to take it out on anyone they could sink their fangs into, rip their claws through. The predators paced nervously around for a few moments, growling at one another but too unsure of this unfamiliar terrain to really go at it. Lions with huge golden manes, tigers, fiercest of the cats with teeth like scalpels, leopards, sleek and quick with slashing claws that could rip a chest open in a flash. They slunk down for a few seconds when they heard the rising roar of the crowd above, their hair standing up, tails falling down between their powerful legs.

But only for a second. Then they saw the women. Instinct took precedence over fear. Their eyes opened wide with a kind of murderous joy that at last they would get something living, something squirming and hot to eat. Not the half-rotted slabs of beef that had been tossed into their cages. They moved toward the women cautiously at first, their eyes focusing in on the cowering, wailing females. Then they moved in for the kill.

The girls from the slave nations, their thighs and breasts showing through their flimsy ripped garments, moved backward as a group. They held onto one another for dear life as if the grip of their neighbor would somehow break the spell of this nightmare. They edged back until they were up against a wall, nearly twelve feet high with no chance of escape. The spectators in the closest seats leaned over the steel wall and jeered them, telling them in no uncertain terms what was about to befall them.

"Get ready to die sweeties."

"I'd like to suck those tits of yours before the cats get hold of them." And other such terms of endearment that increased the women's stark terror. There was no escape. Suddenly they realized it. They prayed to the gods of their homelands— these women from the plains of Africa, the fields of Britain, the forests of Indonesia, the vast mountains of China. Prayed that they would be released from their judgement. But the gods were too far or too busy to hear. Only the cats would be their judges now.

The creatures moved in, nearly thirty of them, their thick shiny fur glistening in the afternoon sun that peaked through the Russian clouds above as if anxious itself to witness the spectacle of death. The predators circled in on the screaming women, no longer concerned with interspecies rivalries, acting now with an instinctive hunting cooperation. They came in from the front, and from each flank, not allowing a single one of the massed group of flesh to make an attempt at escape.

One of the leopards made the first move, a beautiful creature with stark black spots dotting its rich golden coat. It moved in a blur faster than the human eye could capture. Its five-inch-long incisors, created by evolution to sink deep into its prey, dripped with the juices of its hunger. The leopard tore into the front ranks of the hysterical women and sank its fangs deep into the neck of a teenage black girl from the Mlawi tribe of East Africa. The ivory teeth found the arteries, severing them with one bite. The girl fell to the dusty arena ground, the leopard holding tight, squeezing ever tighter with its iron jaws. Her blood vessels torn, hot red blood pulsed out down over her shiny black flesh. But mercifully for her it was over almost instantly. The leopard was a quick killer unlike the lions and tigers who preferred to play for a while with their prey—like a cat. The leopard dragged the twitching corpse backward, away from the crowd, searching for some shade where it could gorge itself in peace.

As if the kill of the leopard was the signal to attack, the other predators charged forward like an army. Each one singled out its particular meal, drawn to them by some unknown internal process of food selection. An immense tiger, nearly five feet high at the shoulder, rushed at a buxom white Irish girl with skin as fair as a first November snow. But it wasn't a quick or efficient killer. It ripped out one of its plate-sized paws, the claws fully extended like a row of daggers, and slashed her across the chest. Her right breast was ripped from her body like a piece of flimsy paper. The Irish girl fell to the blood-specked ground, screaming like a siren. The tiger slashed again, this time across her softly rounded stomach, ripping deep into the tender flesh. The five claws dug in nearly half a foot, five scalpels crudely dissecting the human prey. Her intestines and inner organs spewed out onto the arena floor in an explosion of blood and torn flesh. The huge carnivore put one of its paws on the squirming woman's throat and slammed its opened jaws into her oozing innards. It ripped at the red goodies, taking bites of the soft organs—its favorite food—pulling out large chunks of the firm dark kidneys and liver and pancreas. The poor girl was still alive, her heart pumping furiously to sustain her existence. She could feel the tiger tearing at her and knew there was not a thing she could do. Its face red with blood, dripping in little drops from its long white whiskers, the tiger moved up to the skull for the brains—the next item on its list of delicacies.

The other cats tore into the crowd of sacrificial girls like a hurricane from hell, slashing and biting everyone in sight. They ripped heads from bodies, severed arms and legs with single swipes of their razor claws. The roars of the blood-maddened predators mingled with the cries of the dying girls and the appreciative cheers of the Red elite from the stands above. The sun winked out again, disappearing behind a mountainous cloud, dark and purple, a bruise across the repulsed face of the sky. Within thirty seconds of the charge every creature had tasted blood. The girls were pulled from the crowd, dragged across the now blood-soaked ground as if a mortuary had exploded, sending out pieces of once beautiful female flesh into a hideous sculpture of human parts. The big cats bit at the still hot bodies, pulling out huge chunks of face and chest with each snap of their teeth. Some of the carnivores began fighting over a particularly choice piece, one on each side, ripping the screaming victims literally apart at the fleshy seams, pulling arms and legs off the bodies like parts of a doll. Only these dolls spurted blood, gallons of it. The cats bathed in hot red liquid, feeding themselves from the tasty flesh until they were full. Within minutes there was nothing even vaguely recognizable as something that was once human—a butcher shop of human meat.

The stands roared out their approval. Their faces were wide with sadistic excitement, their mouths screaming in demonic happiness. The games were off to a good start. Commissar Dubrovnik let the cats eat for about five minutes, knowing the crowd loved to see the female flesh actually disappear into the throats of the killers. Like the consummation of a sexual act. He knew his audience well—just how long before they became bored. When the squeals of glee from the stands began quieting, he knew it was time to move on.

"Remove the cats," his deep voice intoned over the loudspeaker system. Instantly, squads of lance-toting arena staff wearing black leather uniforms studded with brass at the shoulders rushed out and prodded the predators back to the gate they had emerged from just minutes before. The animals were reluctant to leave their feast, but the sharp tips of the long spears, poking, digging into their thick pelts, persuaded them to leave. But there was little left to be eaten anyway. Carrying the last morsels of their meals, long pieces of blood-slimed intestines and whole skulls in their mouths to chew on later in the confines of their dark cages, the cats submitted to the will of their masters and, growling angrily, moved through the entrance and down into the subterranean tunnels of the arena.

While attendants hosed down the bloody grounds for the next segment of fun and games, hawkers went through the stands selling food and drinks to the spectators. The men of power squeezed their women's thighs and leaned over, biting softly into perfumed necks. They were aroused by the spectacle and could hardly wait to return to their luxurious bedrooms where they would soon play their own games of sadism and sex.

Dubrovnik liked to pace the death games with big and then small events, raising the crowd's emotions to fever pitch and then subduing them again. He knew how to manipulate his charges like a puppet master his dolls.

"Let the gladiators enter," his ominous voice rang through the coliseum. Out came two teams of fighters. The crowd roared with laughter. This was the "humorous" part of the program for the gladiators, if they could be called that, were all the misfits from the streets of Moscow and other Red cities. Dwarves, cripples, armless, legless men — they came out hobbling and stumbling, some on carts with wheels. The wretched of the earth who would have been far luckier to have died at birth as had most such "inferior" mutations. These had had the misfortune to live — but now they would die. They carried equally absurd weapons: carving forks, shovels, boards; one small man with misshapen physique and some sort of scalelike covering on his body carried a woman's high heel shoe in each deformed hand, with long, pointed heels with which he would try to bash in an opponent's head. The wretched ones had been friends — friends in misery, at any rate, within the confines of the vast holding pens deep within the underground tunnels and warehouses of human flesh of the arena. But now they could no longer care, show any compassion. Each was on his own and their continued life could only be assured by the destruction of those around them.

Nearly one hundred of the pitiful specimens of humanity hobbled or rolled to the center of the stadium as the crowd roared with obscene laughter, their faces red with harsh smiles. The bugles sounded again, signaling the fight to begin, and the wretched ones squared off and began their struggle to the death. It was a ghastly show, these cripples who began slamming away at one another with little strength, hammering away with their crude instruments, weapons that would take many blows to kill a man — insuring that death would not come quickly or easily for any of them. A hammer smashed into a dwarf's face, bruising it, smashing the nose flat as a piece of bloody cardboard; a rake scraped down the side of a one-armed man's chest, leaving countless gashes that began oozing blood like thick moisture from a cave wall. The fighters' faces were twisted, screaming, trying to gather all the strength and hate they could muster to give them the ability to kill. Blood began flowing from myriad minor wounds as the high pitched squeals of fear and madness issued forth from the misfits' mouths. Shovel against shard of glass, icepick against tire iron, wooden chair against hammer, one man even swung an ancient rusted iron on a long electric cord, bashing in whatever head he could reach. They battled one another with the ferocity of those who wish only to survive.

The first to die was a man mounted onto a pulley by straps around his waist. He was broad at the top remaining part of his body with wide strong arms. But bound to the wagon he was vulnerable. A dwarf with short stunted legs and a twisted gnarled face out of some madman's nightmare came at the man, swinging a large mallet. The half of a man fought back wildly, holding a two-by-four about five feet long with nails embedded in the end. He caught the dwarf in the shoulder and ripped a huge gouge into the thick flesh. The dwarf screamed and jumped back. But he was no fool. He dropped onto his stomach out of range of the flailing man and edged forward under the wagon. With a push of his short but powerful arms he turned the pulley over, the half man strapped into it, now on his side, scrambling wildly like a turtle on its back. The dwarf leaped over the crumbling wooden vehicle and with one swift arc of his stunted arms brought the iron mallet down on the cripple's head. The skull crushed in like an egg, and brain oozed through the shattered bone. Again he raised it, and again, slamming into the head until it was reduced to a slimy cracked piece of red porridge.

The crowd cheered the first death, and the bugles went off as they always did when the initial killing had occurred. The Red elite swigged happily from their silver flasks, cold vodka burning the throat and bringing a glow to their jaded hearts. Soon, the bodies of the crippled gladiators were everywhere: a shovel brought down sideways by a one-armed bald-headed creature nearly decapitated a short hairy man with one leg. Blades, forks, razors, shoes, wooden stakes all slammed into flesh and skulls, tearing them apart and releasing torrents of red. The fighting raged on for nearly fifteen minutes until there were only two of the wretched ones left: the dwarf with the mallet and a blind man with a long metal scythe that he spun continuously around him. He alone had taken out nearly five of the now dead misfits whose bodies littered the stadium grounds, crushed misshapen dolls. The crowd cheered their favorite on, some rooting for the dwarf, others for the nearly normal-sized blind man, an albino with skin as pale as chalk and platinum hair. The blind fighter continued to spin around, holding the scythe at waist level, ready to take out anyone who came near him. He had no idea how many were left, but he knew he had killed some. He had felt the weapon dig into flesh and the blood splatter across his hands and face—had heard the death gurgles.

But the dwarf hadn't survived this long without some cleverness. He crawled forward on his belly just beneath the whirring scythe, spinning just above his head with a terrifying whistling sound.

With all his might he reached forward and slammed the heavy mallet into the blind man's knee, shattering the kneecap with a sickening snap. The blind fighter fell to the drenched ground, letting go of the scythe as he grabbed hold of his knee, bone fragments piercing the skin like shrapnel. The dwarf moved with the speed of a striking snake. He grabbed the scythe in midair as it tumbled from the man's grasp and leaped to the side of his fallen opponent. With a ghastly scream of power he lifted the long curved blade in the air and brought the tip down into the blind man's chest. The razor-sharp blade buried itself in flesh, going clear through the fallen warrior and into the ground. The body jerked several times, the blind man's hands grabbing at the blade which nearly sliced several of his fingers off. Then he was still as blood spouted up like a fountain from the deep wound.

The dwarf lifted his mallet again and leaped up, searching frantically around for the next opponent. But there were none. Just a charnel ground of mutilation, blood and pieces of flesh. He could scarcely believe it. The crowd began cheering him, standing in their seats, laughing and sarcastically applauding this "great gladiator." The dwarf raised his now blood-coated weapon high in the air and turned slowly, letting the crowd see this hero of the misfits. A twisted smile crossed his thick hanging lips as his narrow black eyes coolly took in the audience's response. He knew he would live. And even though he was a member of the lowest of the low, he would be rewarded for this victory. He would have food and vodka—even women. The Reds rewarded those who were expert at death, even ugly dwarfs like him. Attendants came out and placed a crown of thorns on his head and a purple robe around his shoulders as they slowly led him off. The dwarf cradled the mallet in his dark hand, the instrument of murder that had brought him through this holocaust. He would always carry it with him now. Let any man attack him or try to hurt him and the dwarf would crush that man's skull in. For this one day in his miserable life he was something—something born out of a river of blood.

Commissar Dubrovnik knew his audience well. Even they needed comic relief from the slaughter. "Begin the pageant," he said, the voice booming out through the stadium like the words of God. A God of ultimate blackness. A circuslike procession paraded out through the arena: women in dazzling jewel-covered gowns, baton twirlers, men whirling long shiny scimitars. They came out on foot and riding atop horses, zebras, giraffes and elephants, as Russian martial music pulsed out over the P.A. They formed large concentric circles, dancing and spinning, acrobats performing gymnastics, tumbling and flipping through the air. The crowd watched appreciatively if somewhat bored. Many took the time to relieve their bloated bodies of the alcohol they had consumed while others walked around greeting their cronies, setting up appointments, making deals. For aside from the sheer spectacle and brutality of the death games, they were also a social event at which virtually everyone who was anyone turned out. A time for bribes, conspiracies, as well as death.

After about twenty minutes the pageant exited the arena, and the buglers blew blaring chorus. Now the real games would begin — the event that the blood-hungry crowd had waited for all afternoon: the duel of the gladiators.

Chapter Sixteen

"Let the death challenge begin," Commissar Dubrovnik said over the speakers. At each end of the vast arena, steel gates slid open and the fighters emerged. There were nearly fifty of them on each side. At one end, the famous gladiators, whose names were known throughout the empire, were decked out in a dazzling array of gold and red and black. Some wore all leather with metal studs running down their sleeves, others capes of silk and velvet. They carried their weapons, each a specialist with his particular brand of death from sword to battle axes, lance to mace. Each had killed many times. They had risen to the top on a mountain of dead bodies. They sneered and laughed as the prisoners walked out at the far side of the coliseum. These fools would be short work for them. Even this Rockson would die swiftly under the unstoppable power of the Black Menace who stood at the front of the gladiators, his face motionless, a visage of steel-hard death.

At the other end Rock emerged first, wearing dirty khaki slacks and a leather vest, followed by the slave fighters who had been captured and brought here to die as entertainment for the Red rulers. They were all strong and tough men—after all this was purported to be a real contest. If there was no possibility of defeating their experienced gladiator opponents, there would be no entertainment. And that was what the death games were about: survival of the fittest, the cruelest, the fastest. Some of the gladiators would die today. That was without question. But not many—of that they were sure. The prisoners wore the gray or black loose-fitting pants and shirts the Reds had given them. They weren't supposed to look too heroic. But they had been given real weapons—weapons that, if they were lucky, would rip into gladiator flesh, cut out a heart, pierce a lung. Most had been given a choice of weaponry in their training, and each had chosen the particular form of murder that they felt might somehow give them an edge. Nets and tridents, broadswords, axes—whatever they had chosen at the start of their two weeks of training from a large bin of weapons. Of course many of the instruments were half rusted, dulled. They wouldn't be given much of an edge. But the audience above, growing increasingly excited as the fighters walked toward each other across the wide arena, didn't know that. Couldn't see the dulled blades. From the stands it looked equal—even fair.

Rockson carried the duo-blade in his right hand.

The nearly three-foot-long weapon was not as shiny as the gladiators' glittering tools, but Rock had secretly sharpened the blade on a file that had been slipped to him by his trainer who had quickly grown to admire, even like the freefighter. Late at night in his cell, Rock had sharpened the edge of the weapon until it could cut a hair. It appeared dirty, grimy, but it would slice flesh—if it could make contact. Archer stood near his leader, a long rope net in his left hand, the mud-coated trident, nearly eight feet long in his right. He grinned at Rock.

"We kill," he muttered through moist lips.

"Yes, my friend, we kill," Rock answered softly, praying that when the next few minutes were over, both he and Archer would still be among the living. The rest of the men were in no mood to fight. Their training had been short and, though they were all broad, muscular men, most of them had never been fighters in their life—but farmers, peasants, untouchables picked up by the Reds. They were not ready to die and the oncoming gladiators looked as fearsome a group as they had ever seen.

"Help each other," Rockson said, turning his head around to the prisoners who walked solemnly behind him. "Don't let them fight you man to man. If we help one another, some of us may live. If you kill your opponent help one of your fellows."

"But—is against rules," a burly, bearded man holding a double-sided axe and said, just to Rockson's side.

"Fuck the rules," the Doomsday Warrior responded angrily. "Their rules are for us all to die. Today we begin by changing the rules." His words and his seeming fearlessness gave them all a burst of hope. Perhaps they might survive. This American was a tough man. Even many of them had heard his name out in their thatched huts and small villages. The Doomsday Warrior's name was known throughout the world. As much as the Reds tried to deny his existence, Rockson had become a planet-wide symbol of rebellion, of the ability to fight back against the Red machine—and win.

The gladiators spread out in a wide line, their weapons at the ready. They sneered at the oncoming prisoners. Each picked out his man, pre-chosen by a selection committee of the games. Dubrovnik liked certain weapons to be pitted against others: sword against trident, mace against spear and net . . . It made for good combat and picturesque results.

Suddenly the gladiators were upon them in a flash, rushing into the V-formation of the prisoners, their weapons swinging through the air, searching for skulls, for chests to crack open. Rockson saw the Black Menace coming at him, moving slowly. The master gladiator had no need to rush. He knew the outcome already. He lived to fight, to destroy men's bodies. It was the only time he felt truly alive. Rock held the duo-blade firmly in his right hand with his wrist and arm as relaxed as possible. He knew speed was his only possible response to the overwhelming power of nearly four hundred fifty pounds of black death machine. The Black Menace walked up to Rock, stopping about ten feet away. The Menace had eyes that bore into one's head. His knees were slightly bent, poised to move suddenly forward. The product of genetic experiments to produce a killer for the gladiator pits, he was, if you could consider an overdeveloped half animal murder machine *art*, a pinnacle of genetic rearrangement. Quite handsome really, with the jutting jaw and rows of wolf-like canines, and the third arm protruding dead center from his chest. The Menace held a long spear in his left arm, a short blade for piercing in his right and a thick steel shield in the third middle arm.

As quick as a cat he leaped forward, thrusting the spear at Rockson's guts. But Rock saw the flicker of the killer's eyes and knew the motion was coming. He jumped to the side and swung the sword edge of the duo-blade at the Menace's abdomen. The blade barely made contact as the black gladiator was so well trained he was able to stop his great bulk in mid-stride. Still, Rock's blade drew a thin line of blood along the gladiator's stomach. The Menace pulled back a few feet and looked at the American with surprise. Only two men had ever cut him in his years in the arena. And they had both been among the most famous fighters of their day. That is until the Black Menace had severed their heads.

The towering fighter opened his jaws, showing his rows of razor teeth, and made what Rock could only interpret as a smile, though hardly a friendly one.

"Good—you fight," the Menace snarled. "We have fun together—before I kill you." With that he charged again, both of his weapons ripping through the air at Rockson's mutant flesh. The Doomsday Warrior parried the trident with a quick turn of the duo-blade and then just as swiftly caught the thrusting sword with the hooked end of his weapon, locking it for a moment. But Rock had forgotten about the third arm, not having fought many men with three appendages. The middle arm of the Black Menace shot forward, holding a two-foot-wide shield emblazoned with fiery designs, and caught Rock squarely in the face. He flew backward several yards, feeling himself almost blacking out. But instinctively he hit the ground in a ball and rolled out, coming up in a crouch. His head cleared within fractions of a second, just in time to see the genetic monster coming at him, the trident flying toward his throat. Rock dove forward, straight between the Menace's towering legs, and sliced one thigh as he slipped right under the gladiator. He turned on a dime as he came out behind the black master of death and held the duo-blade at the ready. The Menace stabbed at empty air and then felt a sharp pain along the inside of his leg. He looked down. He had been cut—deeply—and Rockson had disappeared again. No matter. He turned as Rockson awaited the next blow.

Around them the gladiators tore into the prisoners, ripping at them, tearing through them like a hurricane through a stack of bowling pins. Pins that screamed and bled. Within the first sixty seconds nearly a third of the prisoner-fighters were dead, their mutilated bodies lying stacked around the arena dirt like so much firewood. But the rest of the fighters stood their ground — the bravest, the toughest of the lot. Archer, armed with his trident and net, faced a man nearly as large as himself, armed with mace and bullwhip. The man was a stocky Russian from the steppes of Siberia with a face filled with a thousand scars. Hardly any of his original features remained — just a patchwork quilt of red and purple streaks and cuts and gashes. He charged at the freefighter, snapping the whip and catching Archer on the side of his face, drawing a deep cut. But this only infuriated the American, and with a roar he flew forward, right on top of the Red gladiator, knocking him to the ground. The Red tried to lift his spiked mace and caught Archer a glancing blow on the shoulder which the big man shook off. Archer dropped on top of the Russian, forgetting his weapons, and slammed his huge head into the man's face. The gladiator screamed in pain as his nose and teeth shattered and swung the mace again, this time catching several of the spikelike teeth in Archer's back. With a grunt of disdain the freefighter whipped his head down again and again until the Russian was still — the front of his face no longer a face but a mass of crushed bone. One eye hung lazily out of its socket and plopped down onto the blood-soaked dirt as if looking for a hole to hide in. Archer rose, grabbed his weapons and tore into the fighting crowd ready to help any of his fellow prisoners who needed it.

Rock and the Black Menace squared off, circling each other slowly. The black gladiator was more wary now. He knew this was not an ordinary man, not an ordinary fighter. He felt no fear, an emotion he had never known—just caution. He would win of course, of that there was no doubt in his mind. For he had many tricks up his black sleeves. Rock hefted the duo-blade at chest level, moving it slowly from side to side, ready for whatever plan of attack the Menace chose. He had decided from the start to let the genetic monster attack—he would counterattack. The man knew too much for Rock to go in. Besides it was *his* job to kill Rockson. Let him try—let him make the first move.

Above them the stands were in pandemonium. They were thrilled by the bloodiness, the violence of the battles below. Safe in their plush seats they could watch the death games with pleasure. They were somewhat surprised at the abilities of the prisoners, especially the two Americans. Already six gladiators—some of them quite famous—Ivan the Blood Letter, Notov the Terrible, and Rodor the Brain Smasher, lay dead on the ground, their own bodies ripped into pulp. And even the Black Menace seemed to be having a little trouble. But it only made the games more exciting. If the prisoners died too quickly, where was the fun? Dubrovnik must have planned it this way. They could always count on him for a surprise or two.

The Black Menace watched Rockson, checking carefully for any weakness. The man was strong. He moved like a cat. But somewhere there was a vulnerability, an Achilles' heel. Suddenly the Menace feinted to the right with his sword, and as

Rockson responded, he twisted and came at the American's side with the pike. The razor-sharp tip grazed Rock's ribs, gouging out about half an inch of flesh but not penetrating the rib cage. As the weapon slid past his body, Rockson lashed out with a sidekick to the Menace's groin, catching the black warrior squarely in the testicles and lifting him nearly a foot off the ground. Even with a steel-plated groin cup beneath his black leather pants, the kick took the wind from the Menace. He landed sitting, his weapons falling to the side. Rockson moved in instantly, slashing with his duo-blade with the hook-tipped end at the black killer's throat. But the ebony gladiator was nearly as fast. He whipped his head to the side, and the hook dug into his left ear, ripping it from his head. A flow of hot blood washed down the side of his face and neck. He slammed up again, with the middle arm still holding the shield, and was able to knock Rockson backward with a blow to the chest. He quickly grabbed his weapons again and leaped to his feet with amazing grace for such a large man.

Now he was growing concerned. No one — ever — had hurt him like this. The ear could be sewn back on — that didn't bother him — he was not concerned about his looks. But the sheer fact that the American could inflict such damage was quite a shock. He would have to use one of his tricks, something he rarely did, preferring to rely on his own innate abilities. But survival was the name of the game and Rockson must die.

Rock glanced over to the warriors battling it out just yards away. The clanking of metal against metal. The sudden scream of a man whose life had just ended. Archer was wreaking havoc, a huge mace attached to a long chain in one hand and a five-foot-long curved sword in the other. He waded through the gladiators like an elephant through a forest of trees, whipping the weapons through the air, cutting off hands, smashing in skulls. He was tipping the balance to the prisoner's side, and they fought with increasing vigor, suddenly realizing they had a chance.

Rock quickly turned his head back toward the Menace who was circling to the left now, moving rapidly, trying to tangle Rockson's feet up. The black warrior opened his jaws wide, showing the freefighter the rows of teeth that could shred a man's face with a single bite. Rock sensed that the motion was to distract him and, detecting a sudden movement from the arm holding the pike, he dove through the air to the right, the opposite direction of the Menace's circling. As he leaped the gladiator pulled a small trigger at the bottom end of the pike, and a small explosive charge situated near the other end shot the spearlike tip of the weapon straight forward — a projectile of steel death. But the Doomsday Warrior was already gone. The bolt shot forward at two hundred miles per hour across the stadium grounds, slamming into the back of Qatar the Chest Opener. The bolt pierced clear through the gladiator, exiting out through his chest with little globules of dark red heart tissue coating the tip. Qatar fell to the ground stone cold dead, much to the delight of one of the prisoners who had been only seconds from death. The prisoner turned and joined his comrades in their increasingly successful struggles against the ranks of trained killers.

The Black Menace growled with rage. Even his tricks weren't working. He let out a bellow of anger and, throwing caution to the wind, charged at Rockson, all of his arms moving at once, a cyclone of steel death with just one target in mind. But in anger he was forgetting himself. Rock's mutant senses gauged the angle of all the weapons as they came in at him. He ducked suddenly down so that he was inside the Menace's flailing reach, only inches from the steel-hard black flesh. Rock jumped up just as quickly and ripped the hooked end of the duo-blade into the black mutation's throat. The hook slipped easily inside the thick neck and deep into the windpipe and jugular vein. Rock pulled the shiny blade out, ripping with all his strength, and it emerged hooked around the artery and breathing tube. As he pulled back, the two fleshy tubes that gave life burst in half, and blood sprayed over his face and chest. The Black Menace dropped his weapons and threw his three hands over the gaping wound in his neck. He tried to scream but couldn't as his larynx hung by a thin veiny tendril nearly down to his shoulder. He staggered backward, looking at the freefighter in bewilderment. His legs trembled violently as they tried to hold up the nearly quarter ton of weight. Rockson stared at the gasping genetically bred mutant and wished it had all been different. The man was cruel—but brave, too. If he had been with the freefighters he would have made a hell of a warrior. But such was not to be.

The Doomsday Warrior swung the knife edge of the duo-blade around with a sudden and powerful slicing motion. The edge tore into the bloody throat and clear through the neck. The Black Menace's eyes rolled up as the head, cleanly severed from the body, toppled and slowly, as if in a dream, fell to the ground. Somehow the body stayed standing for nearly three seconds before it, too, toppled over like a century-old tree struck by lightning. It slammed into the red-caked mud, the three arms twitching in death spasms. Then it was still. The most feared of the gladiators had met his maker—and destroyer—in the form of Ted Rockson.

Chapter Seventeen

Boos and hisses poured down from the stands in a tidal wave of anger. The Master of Death was dead. The gladiators were being mowed down like so many pigs led to slaughter. Rockson joined Archer and the remaining prisoners in their winning battles against the "unbeatable" gladiators. Nearly half the gladiators lay dead, strewn around the stadium ground, their life's blood pouring from their skewered bodies. Of the original fifty prisoners, two dozen still stood, many wounded, their flesh coated with their own and their opponents' blood. But they fought on, made bolder every minute by Rock's success against the Black Menace and Archer's smashing weapons that seemed to take out a gladiator with every thrust. The warriors who had just minutes before seemed so fearless were now falling back, panic on their faces, eyes wide with the growing realization they might well die to a man. Never had such a thing happened in the fifty-year history of the death games.

Rockson carried the dead Menace's sword in one hand and his duo-blade in the other. He waded into the thick of it, slashing at every gladiator in sight. Archer glanced over from the midst of a group of three opponents who had surrounded him and yelled out to his leader and mentor.

"Rooockson, Rocksooon!" A big smile crossed his blood-stained face. With a gigantic sweep of his long, curved scimitar, he took out two of the gladiators at once, their chests cleaved nearly in half. They fell to the ground, joining their quickly cooling comrades, and the third man, a fighter whose face had filled the cover of *Blood Warrior Magazine* just months before, walked slowly backward in terror at this madman of extraordinary power who mowed down gladiators like blades of dry grass. He didn't see Rockson coming up behind him. The Doomsday Warrior tapped the red-helmeted fighter on the shoulder.

"Looking for me?" he asked with a thin smile. The gladiator swung his battle-axe up through the air. But it wasn't quick enough. Rock's duo-blade slammed into the fighter's stomach, going in nearly a foot and severing the backbone. The once famous face turned ghostly pale, and he slumped to the earth, gurgling blood from dry lips as Rock pulled the blade out.

The gladiators fought on. They had no choice. But the tide had turned. The prisoners fought like men possessed. They would live — it was those who had tried to destroy them who would die. The mopping up took only minutes. The final remaining eight gladiators, sensing their impending doom, made a break for the gate, but it was locked. No one escaped, not even those who had made their fortunes on death. The crowd of prisoners, their eyes blazing like exploding novas, closed in. When they stepped back, eight bodies spouting streams of red fell to the ground.

The stands erupted in pandemonium. Bottles, cups, even pieces of chairs were flung down by the enraged crowd. It was not just that their champions had been decimated, not just that their day of fun and games had been rudely interrupted by victims who did not wish to die on that particular afternoon. Worse—it was a defeat for the power of the Red Empire itself. That slaves, half-breeds, renegades, mere peasants, and untouchables could defeat the strongest men in the empire—it was unacceptable, impossible—yet it was true.

Dubrovnik's voice boomed down from the colossal speakers. "Calm down, my comrades. I assure you these men will die soon enough. They will suffer all the torments of hell." But the crowd would not be assuaged. They continued to roar out their disapproval, their hatred of these ragged victors below who raised their weapons high in the air and let out their own bellow of joy and pride.

"Release the cats," Dubrovnik ordered over the P.A. Within seconds the large gate at the far end of the arena opened up and the predators emerged once again, their eyes wide in anticipation. They started toward the fighters at the other side, but as they reached the center of the coliseum, they came upon the bloody corpses of the fallen gladiators. Dead prey was a lot easier to catch than living. Even a cat knew that. They stopped dead in their tracks and began eating the presliced meals that lay as if on a dining table around them. It was a carnivore's dream of paradise: so much flesh, organs hanging out of body cavities, ready to be slurped up. They each found their own delectable meal and sat down for dinner.

Rockson turned to the other fighters who stood around him, wiping the blood from their torn garments. He stared at them with a grim, proud smile.

"Comrades-in-arms—we have won." The men cheered. Whatever fate befell them now, they had for at least one brief moment lived as men. "Too long have you been enslaved, used for the evil sport of the leaders who sit up there in the stands sucking their liquor. Freed men, who have freed yourselves with your own blood and pain, I say to you now, we may all die, but let us die as warriors fighting for that very freedom. Join me in killing the real enemy." He paused and turned, dramatically shooting out his arm and pointing an accusing finger at the stands where the elite sat, still stunned by what they had seen. The freed men stared up at the Red audience and their faces filled with anger. They had had enough of being stepped on, used, tortured.

"We are with you, Rockson," Dajinsky, one of the strongest of the freed men said—he who had killed nearly four of the gladiators by his own hand. "What should we do?"

"Use the nets as ladders," Rock said quickly, knowing they had to move fast before the Reds could call in army reinforcements and choppers. "Throw them up over the walls. Then we can climb up into the stands and destroy our real enemies — not these pitiful pawns in the game." He swept his hand across the arena of dissembled gladiators. The men touched hands and weapons in solidarity and grabbed up the five nets that had been used in combat. The nearly ten-foot-long rope weapons were thrown up over the walls that ringed the stadium arena, and the freed men began scrambling up them. The Russian high command moved in a panicked wave, rushing from their seats, confused, crying out in blind fear as the blood splattered warriors came up at them.

A mighty Afghani muscleman carrying a mace was the first over the top. He grabbed the scrawny throat of Drunski, one of the arena guards, and twisted the neck in one violent motion, breaking it. He threw the Red backward over the wall and down to the field below. The crowd was now a mass migration of terror. Generals jumped over the rows of seats, commissars fell, trampled to the concrete aisles by the maddened crowd whose only thought now was for survival — their own. The scattered guards raised their pistols and fired, hitting in their haste the fleeing spectators.

The victorious freed men now knew that they could take on anyone. If they had been able to destroy the gladiators with all their training and strength, the few guards who stood in their way, the fat bureaucrats pulling out their silver-plated derringers and daggers, were hardly something to fear. They waded into the crowd, swords slitting throats like chickens, blades digging deep into caviar-bloated bellies. Rivers of blood began flowing down the stands, making the concrete walkways slippery with the liquid essence of death.

Archer joined in the battle, having replaced his net and trident with a heavy battle-axe—more suited to his slamming style of warfare. He swung the double-bladed shining death tool back and forth at anything that moved, leaving a trail of corpses—Red masters now red pieces of meat, their lips quivering violently as their last thoughts echoed from their fading brains. Everywhere was death, garbed in long black robes with a bony smile on its skull face. Today was its day. So many souls to take into the black beyond—souls that would endure agonies a million times more painful than those they were experiencing now. Souls destined for hell.

Rockson had higher game on his mind than the scrambling crowd. He had heard the ominous voice of Dubrovnik throughout the afternoon—that ultimate assigner of men to the fate of the arena. Now the commissar of entertainment would himself get a chance to partake of the fun and games. The Doomsday Warrior rushed up the long steps of the stadium two at a time, slashing away with his duo-blade at anyone who dared get in his way. Not many did—and those who tried fell, spouting red spray. Rock didn't slow down. He was a whirlwind of death, his purple and blue eyes glistening with the fire of the avenger, the streak of white hair down the center of his black locks splattered with bright red dots of blood, like some sort of painting of doom. He could see the control booth far above at the very top of the stands. As he approached he saw the guards, the personal protectors of the commissar, stepping from a side door, pulling their weapons as they tried to get a bead on him.

It took less than a minute to reach the top as Rockson, running at full speed, went up the stairs like a man possessed. As he reached the top row of seats, he leaped a low iron fence. There were nearly a dozen bodyguards awaiting his arrival. But what they had planned was not necessarily what Rock had in mind. Pretending to come right at them he veered at the last moment to the side and rushed up to the huge window behind which Dubrovnik stared out with fear-stricken eyes. Rockson pulled his arm back and thrust the Menace's trident, which he had picked up half broken from the ground, with all his strength at the window. It smashed into a thousand fragments, shooting shards of razor-sharp teeth back at the commissar, cutting his face with myriad slashes. Rock waited a moment for the collapsed window to fall and then leaped through the opening, his duo-blade held high in his right hand.

"I'm so pleased to meet you," Rockson said. "I've heard such nice things about you."

"Please Rockson, I—I—meant no harm," the cowering Dubrovnik said, edging backward, away from the enraged American. "I—I—was going to let you live. The premier had given orders just to—

to scare you."

"You're the worst liar I've ever heard," Rock said with a sneer. At the side, guards frantically tried to get back in the door. But Dubrovnik had locked it from the inside.

"I beg you—I have a family. I was just carrying out orders. If it wasn't me it—it would have been someone else. And—and I always gave the prisoners a chance. They were given weapons. If they survived they, too, could become gladiators."

"You make me sick, scum. Only following orders. Don't you know those words were said by other murderers like you nearly one hundred and fifty years ago. Men who delighted in torture and execution. It's those who 'just follow orders' who make this world a living hell for the people of the planet. People who want to live their meager lives out in peace. But no—you wouldn't let them have even their pitiful short lives to live. You had to go out and drag them from the ditches and the fields and end their existence in terror and blood."

"Rockson, I am rich." Dubrovnik gulped, blood streaming in tiny trickles down his face from the many glass cuts. He backed off until he bumped against the back wall of the control booth, trying to keep away from the deadly duo-blade, so coated with blood. If he could just reach his desk and the pistol inside.

"I will give you anything you want. You could be powerful here in Russia. A man like you. We respect power—and courage. I promise you that—"

"Shut up," Rockson snapped. "I don't want to hear any more of your lies. You make me want to vomit. Just look out your window at the graveyard below. It's all your doing—every man there owes his fate to you." Dubrovnik made a leap for the desk and ripped open the drawer. He pulled the revolver out and raised it. Rockson would die now. But the Doomsday Warrior was too fast for the overweight, jowled Commissar. With a powerful leap he flew toward the Red, spinning the duo-blade at the face that had made so many tremble. The pistol was at chest level and Dubrovnik's finger was tightening on the trigger when the hooked end of Rock's blade tore into the commissar's face. The tip slammed into the Red's right eye, cutting it in two and then continued through the optic nerve deep into the brain. Rock pulled the duo-blade out, taking the bloody eyeball with it, hooked like a squirming worm on the tip. Dubrovnik's pistol went off, hitting a guard who was just climbing in the window behind Rockson, sending him flying backward onto his comrades. The Red torture master threw his hands over the oozing socket, now a dripping black hole. His own brain tissue squeezing out through his fingers like a thick paste. He let out one feeble scream and then, his legs twitching in a bizarre dance of death, half hopped several feet toward Rock. The Doomsday Warrior stepped to the side as the hideous dying thing brushed past him. The body took another trembling step or two, and the slashed brain decided it was dead. The commissar slammed across the broken window frame and fell dead as stone, his three hundred and ten pounds of flab draped over the sill.

Rockson turned toward the window and the waiting guards outside who held pistols and swords nervously in their sweaty hands. With the duo-blade in one fist and the dead Dubrovnik's pistol in the other, he walked calmly toward the greeting committee.

"Comrades—fuck off," Rockson said with a commanding tone. "Your master is dead. No one has to know whether you fought me or not. Run! Run now and I'll let you live." There were nearly a dozen of the heavily armed bodyguards. But they had seen what this tornado of fury and violence could do. Their master was gone. There would be another master—and they would serve him—or they could die here on the charnel grounds of the blood-coated stadium. They looked at one another with cowardice showing in every eye. Then without a word they made their decision, and turned and ran down the slimy steps. Rockson let a thin smile cross his tight lips. So much for Russian heroism.

The Doomsday Warrior tore back down the wet steps of the coliseum, row after row of bodies slumped in their seats, vodka and gin flasks hanging uselessly from the pockets of their thick fur coats. He joined Archer and the freed men below. But most of the grisly work had been done. Nearly a hundred of Russia's top echelons of leadership lay dead or dying, packed atop one on another in the narrow aisles between the curving rows of seats like sardines in a net of death.

Suddenly, as if they knew their work was done, all the fighters stopped and turned toward Rock. Archer raised his splattered axe high in the air, as if saluting the gods who watched transfixed from the silver clouds above, and let out a primitive roar of triumph. The other freed men joined him. They, the victims, had become the hunters — and they had left a mark that the Russian Empire would not soon forget.

"We're finished here," Rockson said. "We've got to move. They'll be sending everything this side of Vladivostok. We wouldn't have a chance with just these weapons." The Doomsday Warrior turned and ran down the slippery steps toward the arena grounds where bodies still lay, the big cats chewing on them furiously. He scrambled back down on one of the nets draped over the wall and down onto the damp ground. Archer leaned over the edge and didn't even use the net, dropping with surprising agility twelve feet to the ground. The fighters hesitated just behind him, looking down at the lions and tigers, cheetahs and leopards, their bloody jaws pumping like machines over their half-eaten prey.

"They're eating din-din," Rock yelled back up to the somewhat fearful men. They had faced the gladiators but tigers — that was different. "I swear to you they couldn't be less interested in you right now. Cats always stop and eat when they kill — law of the jungle. We can walk right by them as long as they don't think we're trying to steal their catch." To prove his point Rock started across the field of living death, keeping a safe distance from the predators. They glanced up with wary eyes but kept chewing.

The faint roar of approaching Russian helicopters—and from the sound, a fleet of them—quickly convinced the timid to rush down the nets and run across the field. A few of the cats jumped to their feet as one of the men got too close, but the quick flash of a sword quickly dissuaded even these kings of the jungle to back off and return to safer entrees. The remaining eighteen men followed Rockson through the dark opened gates and down into the winding tunnels and pathways of the subterranean world of the coliseum. Rock tried hard to remember the turns and doors that led up the surface. He made it a point, from years of mountain fighting, to memorize the route out of any area that he entered. An occasional guard or bunch of arena attendants tried to block them, but Rock and Archer in the lead ranks smashed on through without even stopping. After many minutes of running at near top speed they came to a sharply sloping ramp and burst through a low gate and out into the wide avenue that ran past the front of the stadium.

Special Riot Police cars were pulling up, but Rock and the freed men were upon them before they could even raise their big Togar Assault rifles. The evening sun chopped like a red fist into the buildings that towered around them, golden spires, twisting spinningly into the deep blue sky. The men ran down a side street as night fell, darkening the pavements and creating a maze of shadows from the roofs above them. Many of the streetlights were out in this part of Moscow—the poorer members of the citizenry lived near the coliseum. It was considered declassé by the Red elite who preferred the other side of town with its hills and lawns and sprawling mansions.

Thank God for Russian inefficiency, Rock thought, as they ran down one narrow street after another, disappearing into the southern ancient sector where the buildings were delapidated and crumbling and the darkness almost total. Behind them they could see whole migrations of Red choppers roaring around, searching for the men who had made a monkey of Russian power. Every cop, riot squad, army patrol, and elite special forces unit would be looking for them—and wouldn't rest until they were caught.

Rock prayed that he wasn't leading them all into a death trap, perhaps just around the next corner. His sixth sense told him there was something ahead—people—a few of them waiting. He held up his hand and the men behind him stopped. Rock put his pistol around the the corner building to see if it would draw fire—none. He carefully edged around and looked.

"Rockson, man, we was buzzing out about your arrival schedule," Yuri Goodman said. "It was name that tune time." Rock let the gun drop with a laugh.

"So you old jazz masters heard the news?" he said across the alleyway.

"Man, the whole town is jumping with the jive of your performance over at the coliseum," Yuri said. Rock and the freed men walked over to the jazz king and his small band of dissidents. They stood nearly two feet shorter than the fighters, and with their long black robes, pasty white faces, and immense gray-black eyes, they looked like some sort of Snow White's Seven Dwarfs—from an insane asylum.

"Let's split the scene," Yuri said, turning and pointing to an almost hidden manhole cover, layered with dust and grime. Two of his men rushed over and lifted the steel covering with two long hooks. "Take a trip on the A Train, daddy-o," Yuri muttered and descended down a narrow metal ladder. Rock and the freed man followed the quickly moving dissident. Anton Coltrane, one of the jazz men who always took up the rear, took a final darting look down the street. Soldiers were drawing closer, just blocks away, but they wouldn't find this. He slammed the cover closed, invisible in the night darkness, just a crack in a street of dirt and garbage, and scrawny dogs wandering like lost souls looking for heaven.

Chapter Eighteen

The challengers of Russian rule sat around large oval tables in the cool dank night air of the subway, thick with scents of moss and rust, planning how they would attack. They drank cup after steaming cup of fresh coffee and espresso which the dissidents said they had stolen from shipments of Columbian beans sold at a deluxe gourmet store for the top Red brass.

Rockson and Archer would take the Missile Control Complex and the freed men would come with him. They would use the explosives that the dissidents had brought up by the crateload. If Rock could take out even half their atomic weapons with this one punch, it would be a blow heard around the entire planet. The dissidents, meanwhile, would make a move they had been planning for years, but until Rockson's example, had been unsure how to proceed. They would storm the

Moscow prison: a decaying stone czarist-built detention center housing nearly five thousand men. Many of them were political prisoners: artists, writers, and members of the dissident's own force.

"We ready for the biggest jam session ever tooted on the planet," Yuri Goodman said to Rock with a lopsided grin on his chalk-white face.

"With dynamite playing drums," Rock answered.

The dissidents drew maps on a blackboard they had discovered years before in what had been the subway director's offices. They drew long arrows with piercing thin pieces of chalk, showing Rock and his men just how to reach the Russian high-tech complex and the location of the main beams of support.

At last the dawn broke, spitting gobs of pale light through the rock-covered gratings far above. The attackers loaded up with rifles, submachine guns, and dynamite, two-by-three-foot wooden boxes of the stuff—a virtual armory. The dissidents would use their full array of supersonic instruments: clarinets, trombones, flutes, saxophones, even tubas. Each was equipped with a sound amplification system that could kill. It had been invented years before by one of their more famous dissident ancestors—a Nobel prize winner who had been marked for death by the Reds right after the war. He had continued working on his sonic experiments down in the subways until he had perfected the electronically assisted atomic-batteried section with microchips and amplifying circuitries. The normal sound of the instrument was phased much in the same way that a laser puts all light waves in synchronous flow. All this scientific jargon meaning one thing—it could kill—kill violently and horribly with the receiver of the supersound having his body's cells disrupted so violently that, at the instrument's highest output, the victim would melt into a human slime. The dissidents played different tunes, depending on whether they wanted to stun, kill, or destroy. The melodies, having certain melodic structures, notes, and decibel peaks, had been precisely calculated as to what their effect would be. For rats and tunnel creatures they played "Chattanooga Choo-Choo; for rendering Red soldiers unconscious, the "St. Louis Blues;" and for wipeout time they blared out "Take the A Train." These songs had been banned throughout the Russian Empire, as had all jazz, considered a degenerative example of capitalistic music. The Red soldiers feared the tunes, not understanding how they killed, but knowing that a song was heard and then a combat trooper was dead.

"We free the Polits," Yuri said proudly, slamming his small hand down on one of the dynamite crates. "Cats be dancin' in Chicago tonight."

"And Down in New Orleans," Rock added, remembering the snatch of song from an old Century City archive record. Rockson and his team loaded the wooden boxes filled with explosives on their backs and hefted their weapons from the gladiator fights. Only now they carried subs as well, courtesy of the dissidents' stockpile.

They were led down one of the long tunnels,

Archer growing nervous as they traveled through the darkness, remembering his encounter with the subway creature. Perhaps there were more. He shuddered, made sure his crossbow was loaded, and moved into the safe circle of light cast by one of the dissident's round red globe lights that created dancing shadows on the smooth tunnel walls as they walked. They marched for nearly an hour, and the guide, Igor Brubeck, led them up a narrow manhole causeway, through which steam drifted up from large industrial pipes that fed the factories of the city above. The diminutive man pushed up on the steel manhole cover at the top of the ladder with a single thrust of his surprisingly strong arms and led the attackers to the surface.

They found themselves at the edge of an immense industrial park that stretched off in every direction. Here were some of the empire's largest and most complex factories—turning out high-tech metals, alloys, computer chips, lenses, and oil-based plastics.

"The big daddy-o dome is over there," the dissident said, lifting his hand from beneath his long black robe, and pointed a bony finger toward the horizon. The men turned. There it stood, like some impossible ball, a plaything of the Gods, only these Gods carried the power to ignite the world in a ball of atomic fire. The freed men, Rock, and Archer stared at the eight hundred-foot-high dome with consternation. It seemed impossible that they could destroy such a monstrosity of technology. It was a faded gray, ridged with radar screens and telecommunication bowls covering its smooth outer shell like metal warts, in communication with and sending constant commands to its still large fleet of killer satellites and tracking stations high above the earth. A crew of nearly five hundred technicians continuously monitored their courses through the heavens, making slight corrections from time to time. The Reds ruled the skies — through this. If any nation ever got uppity enough to get hold of a bomb or a missile and sent it toward Mother Russia, these sats could detect it and blast it from the sky with a single blast of laser power. This building made them the ultimate rulers of the earth.

Rockson looked long and hard at the huge radar center. He had never seen a structure so dense. It looked like a small mountain, thick and impenetrable. Guards stood on high towers circling the perimeter of the place. It was well protected. Too well, Rock thought, even for these battle-hardened fighters.

"Check you out later," the guide said, descending back down the manhole opening. "And don't play no flat notes." The steel cover slammed shut. Rock and his crew were on their own. They started forward, leaping from shadow to shadow. It was almost two-thirds of a mile to the outer perimeter of the dome, but there was no point in giving themselves away with a glint of steel to one of the tower watchers.

At last they got to within about sixty yards of the darkest outer part of the fenced-in gate surrounding the complex. Rockson motioned them all to get down behind a large grime-coated metal dumpster that had been left outside with the base's garbage. The Reds weren't expecting an attack. There had never been one — not here in such a heavily guarded area. No one would dare. Rock knew the guards would be lax — maybe a little drink or two of burning Russian vodka to keep the chill off a man's back.

"Can you get him?" Rock asked Archer softly, pointing to a lone soldier leaning on the edge of a guardpost some one hundred fifty feet away. The next tower was nearly one hundred yards off on each side. If they could just take this one out and quickly replace one of their own, Red uniform and all, they might be able to enter. Archer nodded without a word, loaded an arrow into his crossbow and squinted down the homemade sights of his deadly weapon. He had taken many a squirrel and duck down at a much farther distance. He relaxed his immense body, breathing out, and took aim. His ham-sized tongue licked quickly across his lower lip as he pulled the trigger. The sliver of steel hurtled through the air with the whisper of death on its spinning head. It buried itself dead center of the guard's chest, and he fell backwards, an instant corpse. Rock edged toward the fence and then pulled himself up over the ten-foot-high link chain perimeter, coming down instantly on his feet on the inside of the military compound. He rushed toward the tower and through the wooden door at the bottom and quickly made his way up the circular staircase three steps at a time. He stripped the dead guard's uniform from him and held it up to himself. Not too bad — the guy was broad shouldered if a little shorter than Rock. But then the disguise would have only to work for a few moments. The guard was a sergeant, Rockson discovered, suddenly noticing the stripes on his inner jacket shoulder. He finished changing, putting the Russian uniform on over his battle clothes. He covered the hole in the center of the breast pocket with the handle of the submachine gun the Red had been holding and then propped the dead man against one of the beams in a leaning position as if smoking a butt — just in case any of the other posts looked over.

He left the tower and began walking casually toward the dome.

The freed men dropped over the fence one at a time, throwing their explosives up to the next man. At last they were all over, even Archer, who nearly toppled the link fence as he lay scrambling on its top for a few moments. They waited in the inner shadows of the tower for Rockson to make his move.

The Doomsday Warrior walked across the open space between the tower and dome, well lit by spotlights that aimed down from the edge of the immense semi-globe, spaced twenty feet apart. He walked up a wide ramp, probably a main loading area, and knocked on the closed steel doors a good foot thick. A camera far above him swiveled toward Rock, and a tinny voice boomed out from a speaker on the wall.

"Orders?"

"Sergeant Vashnikov," Rock said, having looked at the dead guard's ID papers. "A delivery of radioactive tubes for the atomic generators." There was silence for a few seconds. Then a confused voice shot back.

"We have no shipment of R-piping due today."

"Look comrade," Rock continued in his best mumbled Russian. "This guy's got a whole trailer load of the things parked just around the building. These aren't cans of paint."

"The duty commander is not here right now," the voice said nervously from the speakers. "I — I'll let you in. I'll call the unloading teams."

"Thanks," Rock said, coughing so the camera couldn't look too closely at his face. The huge steel doors whirred silently apart and Rockson stepped through. A portly captain sat at a control booth up a set of concrete steps. He waved to Rockson to come into the office and the Doomsday Warrior, his hand firmly on the butt of the dead sergeant, headed up into the office.

"Sorry pal," Rock said as he rushed toward the soldier. He smashed the surprised military bureaucrat on the side of the skull, knocking him cold. Rock turned and looked back into the vast warehouse beneath the dome, filled with row after row of supplies piled high on endless metal shelves. He could see movement far off in the dim flickering lights of the storage terminal. They'd have to move fast. He rushed back to the now fully opened warehouse doors. Rock motioned for the men to come forward. They dashed at full speed across the lighted sector just in front of the dome. They had almost made it when shots rang out from the next tower, to the left of the one Rock had left a cooling corpse in.

"Shit," he muttered as two of the fighters fell. The rest made it in. The Doomsday Warrior pushed the Close button, and the two immense steel doors rolled back until they were fully shut. Outside, rifle butts banged against the metal creating loud, drumlike thuds.

"We don't have much time," Rock said, turning to the assembled men. He held up the map that the dissidents had given him of the plans of the structure's support beams, found in a rotting library years before. "If we can just destroy three of the six main foundation beams," Rock said, going over the plans once again, "the place should come tumbling down." Should was the word that bothered him, but he didn't mention his fears. "We'll split into four teams of four men each. I've shown you how to place the explosives and set them. Any questions?"

"Nyet," the men said in unison. They quickly split up and went their separate ways, having gone through the battle plans nearly twenty times. The Doomsday Warrior's target was the computer complex itself—that way, if they failed to bring down the dome, at least the machinery inside, all of the advanced technology, would be blown to kingdom come. But they also had the farthest route to traverse. He was glad that he had Archer along and two stout-looking fellows carrying rapid fire Lavnikhov-18 subs. Each man carried a small crate of the dynamite over his shoulder, strapped around the back so as to give them movement and mobility. Archer carried two, one over each broad shoulder, and looked as if he could handle a few more.

They made their way through the endless storage terminal, moving just a few feet inside the main causeway, hidden behind rows of unpacked ten-foot-high crates of parts. Suddenly there was a flash of motion and guards were upon them—three Reds wearing the crossed electrical bolts on their sleeves, signifying the Elite Air Force Special Commandos. The men leaped in front of them, blocking their path. Rock and Archer fell to the floor instantly as the bullets of the three Russian subs spat out a storm of metal death. But the two freed men didn't move quick enough. Their bodies were cut nearly in half, and they crumbled to the floor, dripping red bile through dissected body cavities. Rock fired three quick bursts from his own stolen submachine gun from a prone position on the cold concrete floor. The three Reds looked surprised for a moment, and then ghastly expressions crossed their pale faces. They fired wildly from arms that were no longer receiving signals from their dying brains and fell to the sawdust-strewn floor, dead as fallen trees.

Rockson grabbed the explosives crate from one of the dead freed men and quickly saluted them both. Two more unknown soldiers in the eternal war for freedom. He threw the crate over his shoulder, wrapping the homemade harness they had rigged up around his chest. Each weighed nearly a hundred pounds, and the two of them over his back made Rock feel as if he were dragging an elephant, but there was no choice. They needed every bit of "boom-boom" they could handle. He nodded to Archer and they ran like the wind down the center of the terminal. This was no time for subtlety. Rock twisted his head this way and that, one arm cradled around the sub, as they ran searching for more Reds. Far off in the distance he could hear the quick cracks of pistols and then the steady drone of automatic weapons. The others were meeting resistance, too. Just let them get the three beams, Rock prayed silently.

The dissidents, meanwhile, were trekking miles through the decaying underground railroad system with their death-dealing instruments. They pulled flat wooden railroad carriages about twelve feet long, loaded down with dynamite-filled crates, on long ropes that they had tied around their waits. They strained like a team of work horses, singing as they pulled. Two of them in the lead playing out a tune on their trombones at the non-lethal end of the sound spectrum, while the rest sang out in unison.

> "A tisket, a tasket
> A green and yellow basket
> I wrote a letter to my love
> And on the way I lose it."

There were nearly fifty of them, each armed with their own particular musical weapon. Clarinets, trumpets, flutes, tubas hung over their shoulders on colorful straps. Their flowing black robes covered their pasty white bodies. Their thick curly white hair stood up fluffy with sweat beneath their hoods. The dissidents' huge black eyes, used to years of darkness, could see perfectly in the shadows of the tunnel system. They carefully kicked fallen bricks and dead molding rats out of their way as they pulled the two small-wheeled platforms along the rusted tracks.

At last they reached the intersection of five tracks—just above them they knew was the Moscow Prison. The "Hole of No Return" it was called by those unfortunate enough to have been sent there. The prison was notorious for, among other things, its roving packs of man-eating rats that the authorities did little to control, feeling it was fitting punishment for those who were sentenced to the three-hundred-year-old prison. The prisoners would just have to make friends with the toothy vermin. The dissidents stopped the cars just beneath what would be the central hall of the massive confinement and torture center thirty feet above them. They turned the fuses and set the timers on the nearly two tons of dynamite that would bring down the walls of terror forever—for one hour ahead—twelve noon. How many of them would still be alive no man could say. Just as the last timer was being placed, they heard a noise down the track and stopped dead in their places. Every man held his breath.

Suddenly from out of the winding subway tunnel came a wave of black furry bodies—rats—thousands of them. The dissidents swung their instruments around and pulled them to their lips.

They formed a straight line so that their own wouldn't be hit by the sounds and set their instrument levels—to kill. They blew out wild notes, a cacophony of jazz melodies from eons before. The wave of rats stopped dead in their tracks, the first few hundred of the fanged creatures falling onto their backs and kicking their feet in frenzied agony. But the dark, nearly two-foot-long meat eaters right behind them rushed forward, scampering over the twitching bodies. Again the dissidents blew their hot licks. The frequencies lashed out like invisible whips at the army of fur before them. Another twenty square feet of rats flew onto their sides, squirming, wriggling in death agonies. Now the rats slowed. Something was wrong. Their front ranks, the most aggressive of the rat pack, the highest of the rat-pecking order, were dead. A few hundred more made a half-hearted charge as the rest waited back in the darkness, watching. Again, the clarinets, the flutes, and trumpets blasted and again a battalion of rats flopped over on their sides, clawing at the air on the dark roadbed. The fanged army had had enough. They retreated, screaming out high-pitched squeaks of rage and confusion at not having their food.

"Now we kill Reds," Yuri Goodman said, letting his clarinet fall to his side. He led the jazz men up ancient rusting circular stairs until they reached a half-cracked wooden door. They put their shoulders against it, and after several whacks, the moldy padlock on the other side gave way with a snap and dropped to the stone floor. The dissidents rushed through, their sound weapons ready for anything. They were inside a crude rock cell at the very depths of the prison where the czars had once imprisoned their opposition — to die in the dank, lichen covered walls, consumed by rats, bugs, spiders, and fear. A prisoner, his flesh shrunken away to nothing, his bones poking out, was chained to the wall, naked above the waist. Deep red welts covered his back like stripes. He stirred as he became aware of their presence and then looked again, unsure as to whether or not this was just another hallucination of his feverish mind.

"I'm seeing things again," he muttered to himself. He had been in the hole for nearly three years now — a farmboy named Potkin whose crime had been to publish some poetry in a local town paper mildly critical of a local Red bureaucrat. Couched deep in metaphors, it had still been deemed suspicious enough by the Red censors to land him the prison where the only literature had been that of starvation and the whip.

"Not hallucinating. No siree, Bob," Yuri Goodman said. "We the Big Bopper, the Seventh Cavalry and the Chattanooga Choo-Choo all rolled into one." He walked up to the suffering prisoner and aimed his clarinet at the chains that held him, setting the instrument at its most narrow frequency beam. He blew a high note and the metal links broke in half. The man tried to stand on wobbly feet.

"Thank you — I don't know who you are but —"

"No time for regrets, stranger," Yuri said with a smile on his chalk-white face. "We the wild jazz men, the junior birdman of the steppes. Come to free all you crazy jazz lovers here in stone land. Come—we get others."

The dissidents broke the lock on the cell door with a quick note and walked cautiously up the crumbling stone stairs. Every cell they came to they released an amazed prisoner. All seemed to come to life out of their semiconscious states. The taste of freedom did wonders for a man's energy. After releasing nearly sixty of the captives, they reached the ground floor of the prison where the prisoners told them they would have to face many guards.

"No problem," Yuri said to the grimy crowd of released rebels behind him. They burst out onto the vast barred waiting rooms of the prison's reception area.

The fifty or so prison guards, rifles around their shoulders, stood frozen in their tracks as they took in the crowd of black-robed figures before them, lining up in a straight formation. The prisoners cowered behind them, afraid of what was to come and sure that their liberators would soon meet their doom. The scene was frozen in time for a split second, the coats of arms, the long flowing purple velvet curtains, the antique weapons still hanging on the mortared wall as they had centuries before.

Then the tableau unfroze as the guards reached for their Kalashnikovs. The dissidents raised their instruments to their lips and played a single terrifying chord, encompassing nearly every wavelength in the sound spectrum. The notes shot out across the cold stone floor, dropping the guards where they stood. The Reds slapped their hands over their ears, quivering in stunned agony.

"Now we groove, hot babies," Yuri said, turning to the shocked but heartened prisoners. The men grabbed up the fallen rifles of the guards and, with the dissidents in the lead, began making their way through the rows of cells.

Floor by floor they freed every man in the building. It disgusted Yuri and the jazz men to find the prisoners in such a terrible state. They lay in their own feces, skinny, nearly blind, their teeth falling out from malnutrition. Some had not seen light for years and rubbed their painful eyes as they were gently coaxed from their cells. At every floor, guards came at them, ready to kill this absurd band of rebels. And at every floor the result was the same: a quick ultrasonic symphony followed by the instantaneous collapse of the audience. Shaking and drooling, their teeth clamped tightly shut; their brains scrambled beyond repair, the dead and dying guards littered the stairways and floors of the building.

It took nearly forty-five minutes, but with the freed prisoners' help, they finally reached the top cells of the castle and pulled every man from his confinement. The vast assemblage of prisoners gathered on the lower floor and waited for the dissidents to return. They were happy but confused, unsure of what to do next and where to go. Many clutched Russian weapons: pistols, rifles, grenades in their pale bony arms. They were weak but ready to die. At least they would go down fighting. They had sampled first hand the forces of Russian justice and knew there was no salvation — except by firepower.

"We split this scene," Yuri said, addressing the throngs of half-naked, grime-coated prisoners in the main holding area. "We bust out of here now. You go home. Remember it was jazz what saved you." The prisoners raised their arms in a salute of gratitude.

Yuri turned toward the thick wooden doors of the prison, and the jazz men again aimed the instruments at the only remaining obstacle to freedom. They blew. Blew hard — and the wood splintered and crumbled like so much kindling. The prisoners with the dissidents in the lead, stormed through the twelve by fifteen-foot jagged hole in the doors. Outside more troops were lining up at the other side of a wide, rushing moat. The dissidents tore across the drawbridge that was the only access to the prison, wailing away on their musical death dealers. Many of the Reds fell, but some were able to fire before the sound waves reached them. Seven of the dissidents were hit and a dozen or so of the freed prisoners behind them. But the rebels rushed forward and soon were upon the Russian troops. The jazz men moved forward as the prisoners made mincemeat of the remaining soldiers, ripping them to pieces with their hands and feet, with knives and butts of rifles. They left a bloody, butchering yard behind with not a soldier left alive.

In the distance was Moscow, its skyline brightly lit with a million twinkling lights. To the left and right, dark unlit roads that led quickly off into the suburbs and then the countryside of central Russia. The prisoners split up into smaller bands, each heading his own way—back to some wretched hamlet, some pig farm. They might be caught again, but they had already been destined to die. At least they were being given a second chance—a rare occurrence in the Red Empire. And they would be careful this time. It would take many Russians to capture any one of these hardened, bitter men.

The dissidents pulled back about half a mile to some low-lying hills dotted with only a few abandoned buildings. They settled down in the dirt as choppers and armored vehicles came screaming in from every direction.

"Good, man," Yuri Goodman said to the closest jazz man, Vantrov, the saxophonist. "They all going to get in on the sound." He pulled out a small pocket watch with a Mickey Mouse face in its center. "Mickey says—right nooooowwww—"

A roar filled the night sky in front of them. Nearly two tons of dynamite went off at once, ripping the guts from the bottom of the three-century-old castle of one hundred thousand deaths. The walls blew out on every side at the bottom like a volcanic explosion. Then a ball of flame shot out from the square stone windows and the roof, tongues of fire hundreds of feet long, lapping out into the cool air. Five choppers that had been hovering overhead were engulfed in the tidal wave of fire. They dropped down onto the burning roof, exploding in five quick blips of smoke, hardly visible against the rising hundred-foot sheets of yellow that reached up toward the very clouds. Thousands of bricks and chunks of rock showered down into the gathering fresh troops and vehicles below, smashing them into bony goo, covering half-tracks and transports with blankets of red-hot rubble. Screams could be heard everywhere as the wounded tried to struggle free of the conflagration. Secondary explosions began going off throughout the prison as flames made contact with stores of ammunition and artillery shells. Suddenly the entire castle seemed to shake as if in the grasp of a giant. Then a deep sound boomed out as if the very earth was moving. In slow motion the entire castle, nearly five hundred feet high and a thousand feet on a side gave way. The structure collapsed from the bottom first, the walls giving in, squashed, unable to hold the weight above them. Then like a falling house of cards, the bricks and thick mortared squares exploded out in all directions. Within seconds the Moscow prison disappeared from the skyline, falling into a vast mound of burning rubble. Flames and bursts of ammo continued to shoot out from the wreckage, burning in the night like a torch of doom for the Russian Empire.

"Hey man, this gig is over. We got our own tunes to play," Yuri said.

"Good show," Nikov, the tubaist whispered softly, his immense instrument balanced on one shoulder. "Best damn music I ever heard. Coltrane would be proud."

Chapter Nineteen

Rockson peered through the frosted glass square window in the center of a steel door. He could make out shapes moving around inside. He and Archer had made their way up ramps, halls, and stairwells—more than he could count—but according to the dissidents' maps they should be at a side entrance to the main control center. Far behind him he could hear the firefights erupting. He hoped that the freed men would not be wiped out. Death had to mean something—then a man could give up his life with satisfaction in his soul. There wasn't time for games, and Rockson knew he couldn't bluff his way into this room—not with the fighting going on. The technicians and guards inside would know about it by now. They would have to go the more primitive route. Rock took out five sticks of dynamite and bound them together with some tape. He placed the deadly package at the base of the two inch-thick door and set a timer for thirty seconds. He and Archer tore ass around a bend and waited. Thirty seconds later an explosion rocked the halls, shaking the floor and sending out billows of acrid smoke. They rushed back down the corridor and through the curtain of gray. They were inside the Main Control Complex of the dome.

The freefighters found themselves at the edge of a vast, curving room. The ceiling must have risen nearly three hundred feet above the floor, curving like the sky itself. Everywhere computers were clicking, machines beeping out information. Clear sheets of plastic almost forty foot square had maps of the earth printed on them, and the orbital paths of the satellites that circled the earth were clearly demarcated by flashing dots of light tracking their every movement. Radar screens, glistening stainless steel telecommunications equipment, video screens filled with images of earth transmitted back from space all filled the floor and walls of the complex. The internal area was surely the largest man-made structure Rock had ever seen. He whistled through his teeth at the sheer spectacle of the most advanced technology on earth. Even Archer seemed impressed, his mouth dropping open, his eyes scanning the high-tech gadgetry of the complex.

Nearly five hundred technicians clad in white smocks and wearing masks to keep their own human germs and dust away from the array of equipment turned and looked at the wild-eyed freefighters, weapons in hand. There was total silence for a moment as the two groups of men, enemies beyond comprehension, took each other in. Then all hell broke loose. A squad of guards armed with subs came rushing down from a walkway that surrounded the inside of the dome, about fifteen feet above the antiseptically white linoleum floor. Their bullets dug into the tiles where Rock and Archer were standing. But somehow the two Americans had disappeared—Rock diving to the right, Archer to the left. Acrid smoke still rising from the blasted door gave the freefighters a bit of camouflage, at least for a few moments. But Rock knew the odds weren't too good—their few weapons against an advancing squad of Elite Commandos. He'd have to even things up a bit. The Doomsday Warrior reached into one of the crates of explosives around his back and pulled out six sticks. Each had six-inch fuses. Rock lit one with a lighter the dissidents had given him and heaved it through the air at the charging guards. They didn't even see it, coming through the smoke and dust. A roar filled the vast domed futuristic complex, and six Red elite soldiers went flying through the air. Rock didn't wait for the smoke and the falling flesh, like red snow, to settle but lit two more and threw them forward. Another set of explosions ripped the control center, shattering computer screens, knocking down two of the flashing sky-maps from a wall. Another ten troops bit the dust, flying off in all directions as if tossed by a tornado.

Archer, some twenty feet away from Rock, saw a lone marksman high above them on a second platform that circled the wide floor nearly a hundred feet up. The man was drawing a bead on Rockson. He swung his crossbow around and sighted up in a second, used to quick shots from his years of stalking and hunting game and predators, when a single second was often the time difference between living or dying. The sliver of steel-tipped hunting arrow tore through the smoky air like a living thing searching for a home—a home of flesh. It caught the would-be sniper in the right shoulder, spinning him around like a top, until he hurtled from the high walkway and plummeted down onto the white floor, splattering it bright red.

The two freefighters rose to their feet, Archer with his crossbow ready for all takers, Rock holding several sticks of dynamite, the lit flame of the lighter in the other hand, only inches from the fuse.

"Anyone want to try?" he asked the shocked tech squad who sat motionless in their seats, not wanting to believe the carnage that was occurring around them. They were not fighters but technicians, scientists, so clean and unsullied in their white lab coats. One of the techs, with a distinctive red star on each lapel, stood up from his desk and yelled across the floor to the intruders.

"You have no right to come in and cause such damage. This is an important military instal—"

"Save it for the KGB," Rock shot back. "You Russians gave up all your rights when you invaded my country—America. You've heard of it, no doubt?" he asked mockingly.

"But you can't destroy this complex, it's—it's—" the manager of the shift struggled for words.

"Maybe I can, maybe I can't blow it up," Rock said with a razor-thin grin. "But I'm sure going to find out." He glanced at the watch he had taken from the dead sergeant, now coated with dust and blood specks. "Comrades, you have exactly thirty seconds to get out of here, and then I start tossing some of these joy-sticks around. Now move!" The techs sat glued to their seats either through obstinance at seeing their little futuristic kingdom blown to shreds or from fear. Who could say? Archer fired an arrow across the floor which embedded itself in the shift manager's desk, just inches from his chest. That seemed to do the trick. The techs jumped up from their consoles and flickering display panels. In a speedy migration they fled past the two freefighters and out the door. Not one made a move at the Americans.

"We sure know how to empty out a party, don't we pal." Rock grinned at Archer who snorted back. The two of them looked around at the now empty complex, the machines spinning merrily along without their human attendants. Then they got to work. They dragged the crates of explosives across the floor setting five, ten sticks at a time under terminals and behind screens. It took only about five minutes until nearly every unit in the place had something ready to blow it to the dark heavens. Wires led from each group of explosives to the center of the room where Rockson attached them all to a timer set to detonate in fifteen minutes.

"Let's go," the Doomsday Warrior yelled to Archer who carried his crossbow aimed straight ahead at whoever was fool enough to get in their way. They tore back down the corridors and stairs, hearing gunfire coming from all directions. At last they reached the main storage terminal on the ground floor and stumbled right into a fierce firefight between the freed men and a squad of guards. There were just seven of Rock's attack team left, all that remained of the three groups who placed the explosives at the foundation beams—or so Rockson hoped—and they were about to be decimated as they hid behind packing crates. The guards closed in with a stream of automatic rifle fire. But they didn't see the two freefighters coming in from their right flank. Archer let loose with an exploding magnesium arrow into the center of the advancing Reds. The arrow hit the leader in the chest and erupted in a fiery spray of lungs and heart. Rock let loose with his sub, spraying it at waist level across the Elite Air Force Commandos. They fell like so many blades of red grass, clutching their torn guts, and fell to the floor gurgling the last words they would ever speak.

From the other end of the warehouse terminal more and more guards were charging—hordes of them from every part of the vast satellite complex. Rockson had kept some of the dynamite inside his officer's jacket and pulled out four sticks with twenty-seconds fuses. He lit them, dropping then down onto the floor, and then motioned for the remaining fighters to get the hell out of there. They made it to the two barn-sized steel doors which still stood, opening out into the early morning sunlight. Rockson, at the lead of the fleeing group, made it out first, quickly scanning the terrain ahead for Reds. Soldiers were scrambling madly around far off at the fence, perhaps thinking another attack was about to commence. The fighters rushed forward, pumping their weary legs for all they were worth. Five Red troops stood by the link fence with two tripod-mounted 55mm machine guns waiting to distribute death to all comers. Only all comers were coming in from behind them. The Doomsday Warrior fired on the run, taking out three of the Russians with one quick burst. The other two turned around, trying to swing their machine gun, but it was too late. The freed men were upon them in a flash. Blades met flesh and bone, and two more Red oppressors trying to preserve the Russian ideals of slavery and greed crumbled to the dusty ground, dead men.

Rock led them through the fence gate just as a small explosion detonated just inside the terminal. That took care of anyone coming out after them, Rockson thought. A cloud of oily smoke oozed out through the door as if searching for more bodies to cremate. They ran quickly into the dense brush several hundred yards from the perimeter of the Satellite Complex and stopped short as Rock dropped to the ground.

"Did you place them—the charges?" Rock asked the freed men anxiously.

"Two of them," Nastronovich, who still carried his short sword from the death games, answered. "The other team was killed before they reached

231

their beam. As to whether or not the Reds will find the explosives or not I —"

But his question was answered by a thunderous explosion. The fighters jerked their heads around at the sound. The mountain-sized dome shook as if it were in the epicenter of an earthquake. Jagged tears tore across the round surface in several places, flames shooting through. Another explosion rocked the very ground that Rock and the attack team stood on. The most advanced technological structure in the world seemed to tremble violently for a few seconds and then began its descent. The entire left side of the eight-hundred-foot-high globe tilted lazily over one side as if drunk, hesitated for a moment, looking for a soft place to land and, finding none, barreled down at full speed. It took only seconds to bring down what it must have taken the Reds a decade to assemble a century before. The entire white/gray skin of the complex was instantly riddled with rips and tears everywhere, flames licking through like greedy yellow tongues. The Missile Control Center dome picked up speed as it approached the moist ground and crashed with a thunderous roar, exploding into a fiery snow that drifted down in pieces as far as the eye could see. What had been a towering monument to the supremacy of Russian power was now just burning rubble, strewn wreckage, and charred pieces of human flesh.

"Well, that about takes care of that," Rock mumbled softly to no one in particular. Around him the freed men cheered. Never in their wildest dreams had they thought they could ever strike back at the

Red Colossus with such power. Archer's face was lit up like the proverbial Christmas tree as he watched the conflagration, the flames reflecting off his sweat-covered cheeks. Rockson turned toward the freed men with a solemn expression.

"Time for us to part company, comrades. But it's been nice working with you. Any American freefighter would be proud to have you on their team."

The men were touched by Rock's parting words, and each shook his and Archer's hands with slow finality. They would never meet again, and all the freed prisoners were sure to die within weeks, months, years at most. Yet they had something, something Rockson had helped give them. And they were more grateful for it than for anything they had ever experienced in their measly lives. With the burning dome shooting out billows of oily, plastic smoke, silhouetting the city of Moscow off in the distance, the six freed men set off running at a half crouch toward the forests north of the city. If they could reach the northern steppes, the wastelands that Russian troops rarely patrolled anymore, they might just have a chance.

Rockson and Archer watched the men turn to shadows and then dots as they reached the woods nearly half a mile away. Then the Doomsday Warrior turned to his fellow American.

"Well, now it's our turn, big buddy. But just how the hell we're going to get out of here I don't have the faintest idea."

Chapter Twenty

The three tanks stood like monuments to the power of death in the center of a cracked, weed-covered concrete lot. The top of the line of Russian armored technology, they were each fifty tons of murderous firepower, nearly sixty feet long and bristling with cannons and machine guns. They looked almost beautiful in the purple rays of the quickly falling sun which hovered above the low hills surrounding Moscow like a dark pearl about to plunge back into the ocean of night. The Doomsday Warrior stopped dead in his tracks, hidden in the twisted shadows of low gnarled trees off to the side of the Red Army military installation. Behind him Rock could hear the closing drones of what must have been a fleet of helicopters searching for the men who had caused the Red Empire so much damage on this day of destruction.

"Will you take a look at that?" Rock said softly to Archer who kneeled beside him, his chest heaving with exertion from all the running they had been doing. The huge mute looked on curiously, never having even seen a tank before. But Rockson had, and he knew what they were capable of doing. T-82s — the biggest of the Red mobile arsenal. He had once taken control of a smaller version of this battleship-sized vehicle back in America, and laid waste an advancing Red battalion in search of rebel blood. But this monster! If they could just get inside the tank — and the monstrous vehicle was operable — and if he could figure out how to operate the damned thing, they might just have a chance to get to the airfield to which the dissidents had given him directions, some five miles to the south. A lot of ifs — he knew. But they had to get out of the area. It would be like parade day in Lenin Square within minutes — of that Rockson had no doubt. He had caused too much humiliation to the Reds for them to do anything but send out their entire army to capture him.

The two freefighters edged in slowly toward the motionless tanks. Rockson's keen eyes scoured the perimeter for signs of motion. There, off to the left, the glow of cigarette butts in the darkening air. Voices laughing — at least several soldiers — but they were relaxed, not on alert against an attack. Good — surprise was the attacker's best weapon. At the far end of the decaying lot were long, curved aluminum barracks from which he could hear more voices — a lot. Too many men even for him and Archer to take on. But once they were inside one of the demonic machines, it would be a different story. They moved forward on the run, slipping from shadow to shadow like a fox approaching a chicken coop.

There were just four guards near the tanks: young, green recruits, dragged from God knew what desolate province, to live their lives as pawns in the vast armies of the Red Empire. Approaching to within twenty yards of the guards, Rock motioned for Archer to work silently. The Doomsday Warrior gently laid down his sub on the cold ground and hefted his duo-blade. He rushed forward from the darkness like a leopard on the heels of its kill. The soldiers didn't hear the approaching freefighters until they were nearly upon them. They jumped to their feet, cigarettes falling from shocked faces, and reached frantically for their Kalashnikovs which they had placed at their feet. But knives are faster than bullets at close range. Rock's blade ripped across a stubbly throat and the Red slammed to the hard cement ground, a bag of bloody garbage. Archer jumped between two of the troops and, grabbing a neck in each of his baseball mitt-sized hands, slammed their heads together, knocking both men cold as ice. The fourth leveled his rifle at Rockson, getting off a single shot. Damn! The bullet whizzed past the freefighter but caught Archer in his meaty thigh. Rock leaped across the thick slab of wood the men had been resting on and slammed the tip of the duo-blade into the trooper's chest, piercing the heart, slashing the aorta of the pumping machine. The Russian stood still as Rock pulled the blade out again and looked at him as one must look into the fearsome eyes of an avenging God. Then he tumbled forward, smashing his face into the concrete.

"Move, man, move," Rock yelled to Archer who was touching his leg where blood was beginning to seep through. He hobbled after Rock as the Doomsday Warrior leaped up onto black steel of the front end of one of the tanks. He pulled a lever at the top of the T-82 and it clicked, releasing the hatch. Thank God they had left the war machines ready for action. He pulled open the steel hatch and peered down into the dark innards of the tank. Archer was struggling to get up onto the edge, but his wounded leg didn't quite hold him up for the ascent. Rock reached over with his bronzed, muscled arms and helped pull him up until the immense warrior was able to get a grip. Already Red troops were pouring from the barracks at the other end of the lot. Shots rang out like thin pops in the night as dark bulbous clouds raced overhead, blotting out the crescent moon that hung like a poised sword over Russia.

Rock dropped down inside the control section of the war wagon as Archer stumbled down the ladder behind him, half falling onto the cold steel floor. Rock reached up past his compatriot and closed the hatch. Now they were sealed in — to victory or death. The Doomsday Warrior made a quick perusal of the controls and gulped. The thing was a thousand times more sophisticated than the one tank he had driven. But at least all the control buttons and dials were labeled. He pushed the ignition switch and the diesel engine of the tank roared to life. Lights flicked on at the instrumentation panels and screen all around the ten by twelve-foot-square control pit of the T-82. Rockson quickly went over each of the computerized displays, and the instructions beneath them lit up with dim blue lights. The steering mechanism was similar to the one in the tank he had handled. There were twin rods—one for forward and reverse, and the other for left and right. The handle of the forward control rod had a swiveling grip which apparently accelerated the tank with gradations of speed measured in kilometers per hour—able as far as Rock could figure to reach a top speed of nearly forty miles per hour.

He started the monster forward as he heard shots pinging off the black outer skin of the tank. He snapped on a switch labeled Attack Viewing Screen. That was better—video cameras mounted on all sides of the tank displayed on a five-way split monitor a full three hundred sixty degree picture of what was going on outside and above. The images must have been enhanced with some sort of infrared system because Rock could see the surrounding terrain as clear as day. Red troops were coming in on them, nearly a hundred, and some were heading toward the two other T-82s. He stopped the tank dead in its tracks, satisfied that he could at least drive the thing, and searched frantically for the cannon swivel and firing controls. There—turret swivel. He yelled across to Archer.

"See—button there." Archer got up from the

floor where he had been tying a tourniquet around his bull-sized thigh and looked at Rockson with incomprehension. Fighting he could handle, but controls, buttons, dials, they were things that frightened him — a world of science and machinery beyond his ken. But for Rockson he would try.

"Big boom-boom," Rock said by way of explanation, pointing to the firing controls of the tank's immense 125mm cannon. Archer grunted back, standing over the controls. At least he understood that. There was no way that Rockson could handle everything at once. The tank usually carried a five-man crew, each handling a different facet of the operation of the T-82. Rockson would have to train the giant of a man in about ten seconds how to fire the most complex tank in the world.

"I say go — you push. Okay?"

"Ho-gay," Archer shouted back above the vibrating roar of the tank's engine, proud to have understood the instructions. Maybe it wouldn't be so hard after all. Rock sighted the cannon of the T-82, nearly twenty feet long cannon, swiveling it around until the closest of the two other tanks was centered between two glowing circles in his attack monitor. Men were climbing into the black death vehicle, just pulling the hatch closed. The tank was already screaming to life.

"Push," Rock yelled. Archer slammed his huge thumb on the red firing button, and the tank shook with an earthquake-like vibration. Seventy-five yards away the T-82 took a direct hit, exploding a jagged hole in the armored vehicle. Flames poured out as the tank suddenly erupted into a powerful explosion, her munitions ignited. The big murder machine ripped apart at the seams, sending pieces of white-hot metal off in all directions. Archer let out a growl of satisfaction and looked over at Rock with glowing black eyes.

"Good, very good." The Doomsday Warrior grinned back. He swiveled the turret ten degrees to the right and tried to get a fix on the second tank which was already moving its own cannon quickly around toward Rock. But the American made target acquisition first. In the game of high explosive shells, a tenth of a second could make all the difference between survival and total destruction. The sighting circles hadn't even come together, but Rock could see that the other weapon was zeroing in on them.

"Push man — push the fucking button," he screamed out, and Archer again stabbed forward with his thumb at the far side of the control room. The tank shook again and the shell tore forward, smoke whipping out behind it, a mini-missile searching for its destiny. It bit into the treads on the near side of the enemy tank, blasting them apart in a hail of dust and steel. The tank tipped over on its side just as the Reds got their shot off. But the tree-sized cannon was already facing down, only yards from the concrete below it. The shell tore out from the smoking muzzle and hit the hard ground within a hundredth of a second. The explosion tore a crater into the foot-thick cement, and the back fire shot up into the cannon. Rock could see the other tank shaking wildly inside as electrical systems ignited. The next shell into the computerized feed line erupted. The tank blew up from the inside. One second it was there, the next it was gone—unrecognizable as the death-spewing steel colossus that it had once been.

Archer gave Rock the thumbs-up, and the Doomsday Warrior returned the gesture with his own raised hand. "At least our tank friend's brothers won't be following us," he said, patting the control panel. He swiveled the cannon so it was aiming directly forward and slammed the control rod forward. The tank's two-yard-wide metal treads turned, slamming down onto the concrete. Ahead of them the Reds had formed a defensive line at the edge of the installation, setting up machine guns and mortars. Rock bore down on them like an angel from hell, not even bothering to waste any more ammo. He'd need every bit of it for the journey ahead. The tank smashed into the line of men, grinding them up in its treaded teeth. Blood oozed out from beneath the tank, leaving a trail of red paint on the easel of concrete. The T-82 slammed through a link fence, knocking it down as if it were made of balsa wood, and the tank tore off through the dark fields as flames rose behind it, licking up toward the clouds as if trying to burn the very heavens.

As they plowed through the countryside, Rock took the chance to examine the rest of the tank's arsenal: twin 12.7mm machine guns, radar systems that could pick up air traffic for up to ten miles—and something else—a search while tracking radar and FLIR (Forward Looking Infra-Red TV) with laser guidance and range finder. It was capable of firing, as far as Rockson could tell, ten laser-targeted missiles. Jesus, the thing was a mini-fortress. If he could learn how to use the stuff without blowing them up in the process, they just might make it. Rock glanced over at Archer who stood, his thumb perched just above the firing button, with a wide, idiotic grin on his face.

"Puuush?" he asked through wide brown teeth. Rockson couldn't help but laugh at the seven-foot man, his head squeezed down by the low steel ceiling.

"No, not yet pal—but stay ready." Archer nodded and looked down at the button again as if it were a glowing ruby. He had joined the technological age.

Using the T-82s navigational system, Rockson tore through the fields and forests to the north of Moscow, slamming down trees, ripping through gates and fences as if they didn't exist. Far behind them the lights of the Kremlin and the towering spires of the city twinkled with a million flashes of light. Rock knew that somewhere inside, sitting at thick oak tables, surrounded by wall-sized maps, generals pounded their fists down on the wood and screamed out his name. They wanted him— wanted him bad.

After about five minutes of carefully studying the instrumentation panels, with the tank on auto, Rock was confident that he could at least fire most of the complex weaponry. Whether or not he would hit anything he was about to find out. A ruby red light blinked on and off in the center of the controls—words flashed across a display terminal. His Russian was good enough to understand the message. *Enemy craft approaching at 12 degrees south.* Rock flipped on the air, radar, tracking, and guidance system and didn't like what he saw. A V-formation of choppers, nearly twenty of them were coming in fast. He clicked on the engage controls and a message flew across the panel. *Firing mode on.*

"Archer—get over to that other wall," Rock said, pointing to a second control panel several feet away from him. Archer walked over and again poised his thumb—and waited. Rock watched the copters close in as they dropped from the sky like a flock of hawks, firing their air-to-ground missiles from beneath their black metal bodies. The Doomsday Warrior waited until the panel flashed—*Enemy sighted—Guidance system on—Fire when ready.* He prayed that the things actually could home in on the helicopters on their own since there was no sighting device other than flickering dots moving in above them.

"Fire!" Rockson yelled to Archer who slammed his thumb down hard. The tank quivered slightly as two mini-missiles shot out from small portals on the top of the T-82. They streamed up toward the advancing fleet, little slivers of silver fire, smoke trailing in a tight stream behind them. The laser guidance system automatically guided the missiles in on their targets, hitting two of the lead choppers dead on. Both roared into flame, disappearing from the night sky in flaming balls that plummeted instantly to earth. The shrapnel from their concussion ripped off in all directions, disabling two more of the black helios, slicing one's fuel line which sprayed out burning gas, hitting another's top rotor, severing one of the spinning blades in half. Both of the craft fell from the screen that Rockson watched anxiously. The damn thing worked. He wished he had a few more of these back home.

Small missiles and rocket fire slammed down around the T-82, sending up explosions of dirt and weeds. One made contact with the upper rear portion of the tank. But aside from making the T-82 shake violently for a moment, it seemed to do little damage. The war machines had been heavily armored with double thick titanium-steel alloys. It was going to take a hell of a lot more than a small rocket to take it out. The Reds had never figured on anyone's firing at *them* from inside the state-of-the-art war wagon.

They came to a thick grove of trees, and Rock floored the T-82, hoping it could handle the thick trunks. But the tank smashed through them without hesitation. It seemed capable of almost any feat of strength. Trees shattered and snapped in half as if a bull elephant had gone on the rampage, tearing up the forest in a fit of frenzied madness. They emerged again out onto a roadway. According to the dissidents' maps and Rockson's calculations, he figured it was the main thoroughfare leading to the airport. Time was all important. Once they had MIGs on their tail, with their more powerful missiles, even the T-82 would find it rough going. He turned the accelerator grip on the top of the forward/reverse control rod, and the super tank shot forward, gouging deep tracks in the asphalt two-lane road, cruising along at nearly forty miles per hour. But their reemergence into the open also gave away their position on Red radar screens. The choppers closed in again, barking commands back and forth over their radios which Rock was able to pick up on tank's telecommunications circuitries. The conversation went something like, "Get the bastard!" They swooped down for the kill, dropping from the cloud-covered night sky, the strontium blanket of smog dimly visible high above glowing a luminous green.

Rockets suddenly rained down from everywhere, exploding around the tank. Two made contact. But still the T-82 seemed to survive, although Rock could feel the temperature rising inside from the sheer heat of the blasts. Except for two deep shudders and Archer's wide eyes and growing claustrophobia at being confined in such a small space, the death machine kept right on going. Through his video consoles, Rockson could see two of the choppers dropping low and keeping pace with him. They hovered directly overhead, and a cargo door at the bottom of each dropped open. Whatever they were going to heave down on him, he didn't want to be on the receiving end. Rock set the auto-guidance on the missile system again and yelled across to Archer to fire. As simple as the motion was, Archer seemed to get a kick out of just pushing the button and causing so much effect. He was used to slugging it out face-to-face.

Two more of the laser-guided missiles shot from the tank and headed straight up, making contact with the bellies of the choppers in less than a tenth of a second. Whatever the Reds had been about to release down onto the tank never got there. The helicopters exploded into twin balls of screaming metal and showered down onto the T-82, bouncing off its armored back. Still the choppers left in the formation closed in, sending down rocket after rocket, leaving the road around the T-82 a flaming mass of jagged yard-wide craters. They no doubt had orders to get Rockson or not come back at all. An explosion suddenly lifted the tank nearly off the ground. One of the rockets had made contact with the lower portion of the tank, slamming into the right steel tread, knocking three of the steel teeth loose. A light in the center of the systems display panel flashed quickly on and off, and the display monitor blinked on with the words *Tread hit — Tread hit — Tread hit —*

The T-82 slowed to about half speed even with Rock twisting the accelerator to the limit. But it kept going. He had to steep more to the left now as the tank kept wanting to veer off to the right. But the steel cables that held the treads together had evidently not been severed. The immense war wagon lurched forward, grinding even deeper into the asphalt, this time leaving a plowed trail nearly a foot deep from the torn treads. But the choppers were closing in again — and this time for the kill. Rockson suddenly saw a tunnel ahead. The road disappeared inside a granite hill, and the darkness inside indicated that the tunnel went on for several hundred yards or so. It was time to move. The tank shot ahead into the gouged-out crude rock passageway, and he slowed the T-82 to a crawl.

"We're jumping ship," Rock said to Archer who was overjoyed at leaving the war tank. Rockson set the controls on "autopilot" and then the laser guidance panel to fire at any airborne target that approached within six hundred yards. They'd have some surprises ahead, that was for sure. Rock crawled back up the steel-runged ladder and opened the hatch, quickly jumping out onto the top of turret. Archer stumbled up and the two freefighters hit the road, tumbling over several times. The tank charged forward, dragging its torn tread in the semi-darkness. The choppers waited ahead at the other end of the tunnel, hovering just a few feet above the ground. Nearly fifteen of them—waiting for one.

Rock and Archer tore off toward the mouth of the mountain tunnel, reaching the front just as the first of the missiles from the T-82 shot up. Behind them they could hear explosion after explosion as choppers fell from the sky like meteors, and rockets rained down on the unmanned war machine. Let them battle it out, Rockson thought. Red machine against Red machine. There was a certain irony to it all—an irony that would make heads roll when the truth was finally sorted out.

Chapter Twenty-one

From his top floor window, Premier Vassily could see the fires of the Moscow prison and the Satellite Control Complex burning out of control. Flames reached hundreds of feet in the air, twisting and writhing like snakes as they consumed every bit of burnable substance. Vassily sat in his wheelchair, his black servant Rahallah behind him, impeccably dressed in white suit and spotless gloves. They both watched the fires silently, the premier's eyes tight and filled with hate.

"I should never have trusted him," he said at last, almost in a whisper, as if still not wanting to admit that his gambit to ally Rockson and the freefighters against Killov had gone wrong. He had made few errors in his rise to the top—one didn't make mistakes in the Red hierarchy and last very long. But this had been a bad one. A disaster. The destruction of the prison was a trifling matter, the fiasco at the gladiator games, more of an amusement to him than anything else. The death of Commissar Dubrovnik meant little to him. He had never like the man anyway.

But the Satellite and Missile Control Center—that was another matter. That one man could wipe out the Russian's ability to strike across an ocean, if necessary, at rebels and uprisings—it was unbelievable. The complex would never be rebuilt, he knew that for certain. It had been well kept up. Money poured into it endlessly. But the Russian technicians could no longer create such miraculous structures. Their abilities, their factories to produce the computers, the tracking optical and radar systems were no longer functional. No, it would be bombers and land-based missiles, now already within the slave countries borders. If the need came *they* could still inflict terrible devastation. But it would be harder, much harder. And they would be vulnerable.

He had misjudged things, but Rockson would be the one to pay the price. The Doomsday Warrior was a hundred times more dangerous than Killov. Now he saw it all clearly, like a blueprint of doom laid out before his weary eyes. And Rockson was just one of many freefighters. Perhaps Killov was right. He had tried to tell the premier many times—the rebels were growing in strength and boldness in America. And if this single man was any indication of that power, the Russian Empire was in deep, deep trouble.

Premier Vassily felt tired. Tired to the point of wanting to die. He had faced many challenges and survived, nay, emerged victorious. When he was struck by his opponents, his instinct was to strike back—harder—to destroy those who would challenge him. He felt emotions stirring within his breast that he hadn't felt for years. Poisonous feelings of vengeance, of torture. Rockson would have to pay for this. The American freefighter had made an error, too. For now the Reds would strike back more viciously than anything the Americans had experienced in the last century. The entire planet must know, must be shown, what the penalty was for challenging his rule. Every general on his staff, every American from freefighter to peasant farmer plowing his radioactive field—all would feel the wrath of the premier.

Vassily felt suddenly changed. His poetry books, his long subtle novels seemed like jokes now. It was a game of power and the strongest would win. Survival of the species was always won by the toughest, the most ruthless. Perhaps he should read Darwin. On the endless evolution of the strong over the weak. Yes Darwin—he might get some ideas on just how to wreak his vengeance.

"Rahallah, bring me the *Origin of Species*. It's somewhere in my bookcase in the library." The black servant walked quietly and quickly from the room, leaving the old man and his trembling hands to plots of death and blood and madness.

High above, far beyond the scope of the naked eye, the Russian killer and spy satellites began acting strangely. They had stayed aloft for a hundred years, constantly corrected in their angle, their rotation and orbit. Only a few of the technological marvels had failed, plummeting to earth in fiery balls that crashed into the ocean or an uninhabited forest somewhere on the surface of the planet. But already, with their guidance systems no longer receiving instructions from earth to correct the slight flaws of their trajectories, they were beginning to veer out of control.

Little things at first—a slight wobble, a drop of just several miles from a thousand-mile-high orbit, a blinking light flashing a problem in hydraulic pressure or solar battery collection. But the little things would escalate, would grow, making a mistake of an inch turn into miles. The slight vibration of a speeding-up spin became a violent shaking that would tear the balls and triangles and octagon-shaped satellites apart, sending them into more and more erratic flight paths. They danced madly beneath the stars, mindless pieces of steel and nickel, titanium and fiberglass molded together into a vacuum-resistant package. They were marvels of communication, of tracking, the very top of the ladder of man's mechanical ingenuity. But with all their computers and miles of circuitry and wiring aboard, they had no intelligence, no way of righting themselves. But they knew something was wrong—their internal sensors frantically sent back signals to earth requesting assistance, correction of their obital problems. The air burned with telecommunications as the coded signals traveled down through the atmosphere. But only flames were there below to receive their messages. What had been the dome was now a garbage pit of burning rubble. It would take weeks, months for some but soon they would all drop from the skies, flaming balls crashing down from the heavens. Not one would survive.

Chapter Twenty-two

A long spread-out line of Red troops was marching across the nearly barren fields just to the south of the Military Air Field. Rockson and Archer stood at the end of one of the runways, hidden behind thick thorn bushes as a huge Intercontinental Illyushin transport jet came swooping down just over their heads and touched onto the concrete runway ahead. Its forward thrusters burst into screaming life as it screeched to a halt nearly a mile down the airfield. Behind the two Americans the Russians marched forward, nearly a thousand of them, their Kalashnikovs at chest level, bayonets attached, ready at a moment's notice to fire or send the long blade into American flesh. There was a reward of one million rubles for the man who captured either of the escaped freefighters—direct order from the premier. The Reds looked behind every shrub, examined the branches of every tree, scrambled inside sewer pipes and ditches—not a square inch was passed by. Overhead, choppers flew in concentric circles—all of them searching, searching for just one man—Ted Rockson.

"It's nice to feel so wanted," Rock quipped to Archer. The big freefighter grunted out a noise that sounded like "yes." They had only minutes, perhaps seconds before they would be spotted. Rock had to be bold, move fast—there was nothing to lose. That was clear. Should the Reds get hold of them again their fates would be quite terrible, even for him who had withstood pains beyond human imagination in his lifetime. And this time the new Mindbreaker *would* be used. Even Rock knew he couldn't stand up to that. He might not talk, but his brains would be scrambled like a henhouse of eggs thrown into a bonfire.

"Let's move," Rock said quickly. "This may be our last footrace together." The two freefighters began running down the field straight along the middle of the runway. Their feet slammed onto the hard surface lit up by floodlights posted along the far sides of the field, lighting the four landing beds for the planes that were constantly arriving and departing. Another jet soared down just over their heads with a deafening roar. The wheels seemed to almost touch their heads as the draft of the immense Illyushin, ferrying a shipment of jeeps from a far-flung northern factory, nearly knocked them to their knees.

Just ahead Rockson could see three jets—MIG 99s, from the look of them, sitting just off the main runway. If they could just . . .

Rock felt the whisper of bullets flying past, one just inches from his ear. Above, at the top of the control needle, he could see faces peering out from the tower windows, pointing at the two freefighters, yelling out in confusion. The three MIGs stood in a line, one after another, obviously ready for takeoff. The second two were empty, but the first held a pilot, checking out his instrument panels, fuel gauges, and other functions in preparation for takeoff. His cockpit cover was open, standing nearly straight up as the pilot had apparently just sat down inside the jet fighter.

Rockson felt a sudden sharp sting in his lower back as a Red slug passed clear through the right side of his body. No time to stop and check it. He could still move that was all that mattered. He'd live or die according to the decision of the gods. He approached the jet from the side, the pilot obviously still unaware of all the commotion around him, so intent was he on his flight prep. With a single leap of his catlike legs, Rockson was halfway up the detachable ladder that hung at the side of the MIG. With two quick steps he was at the edge of the cockpit. He leaned over the side, holding his submachine gun in hand, and pointed it at the Red officer's chest.

"Surprise!" Rock yelled out. The pilot turned and his face went instantly pale as he saw the blood-spattered, grime-coated American. He reached suddenly for his pistol, strapped beneath the seat, and drew it up. That was his last mistake. Rockson pumped half a clip into the man, and the

257

body slumped down in the seat, the flesh riddled with countless little red holes, the head falling to one side like a lifeless rag doll. Rock stepped inside the cockpit and quickly unstrapped the Russian. He hefted him over the side of the plane and dropped him down onto the concrete runway where the corpse landed with a sickening thud. Rock sat down in the slanted leather seat and strapped himself in, his back beginning to throb painfully. He reached around and looked. Blood was seeping through the Red sergeant jacket that he still wore. But it wasn't pulsing—that was a good sign. And his spinal cord obviously hadn't been damaged or he wouldn't even be able to move. Maybe he'd make it yet again. Archer stumbled up the ladder, dragging his wounded leg behind him, and dove into the copilot's seat just behind the Doomsday Warrior.

"This is going to be the fastest takeoff in recorded history," Rock yelled around to the gigantic freefighter. "Strap yourself in." He pointed to the seat harness, and Archer, with a look of enlightenment, slammed the small metal clasps together on the belt. Rockson had never flown this particular jet before, although he had piloted several stolen jets over the years. But he did know about its workings. He made it a point to familiarize himself with every scrap of information that came his way on Russian arms and craft. The Doomsday Warrior had spent weeks at the Century City computer screens, going over every captured manual of operations. He had been the first in line to examine stolen Red equipment and documents. Survival in America 2089 A.D. meant knowledge. The ignorant perished like match flames squeezed between the fingers of death.

Rock pushed the Systems On button. He'd just have to hope that all the equipment of the jet was functional. The cockpit cover slowly lowered itself above the two Americans and clicked tightly shut. *Oxygen Systems On* flashed on a computer screen in front of him.

"Put on the mask," Rockson yelled back to Archer who seemed quite confused and unhappy about trading one claustrophobic situation inside the T-82 for another, even smaller squeeze inside the MIG. The seats were not designed for seven-foot-plus four hundred fifty pounders, and the American's legs and knees were propped up behind Rock's plastic-backed seat. The Doomsday Warrior pushed the ignition switch just as the first ranks of Red soldiers got within firing range. The exhaust flame of the MIG spat out nearly one hundred and fifty feet down the runway incinerating those who had been most eager to win the reward for Rockson's head. Dials and lights flashed on everywhere inside the cockpit, lighting up the instrument panel before him, but Rockson didn't have time to contemplate their meaning. He pushed the control wheel, really more of a triangular shape, forward, and the sleek olive-colored jet lurched forward. He headed the craft out onto the main runway as frantic Russian commands snapped over his headset.

"Stop what you are doing! You are not cleared for takeoff," a gruff Russian voice bellowed over and over. Fat chance, Rock thought. He could see the rows of troops shooting at him from down the runway, their bullets whizzing all around the jet. An occasional slug ripped into the side of the MIG, but it was armored as well, plated with alloys to survive shots from 55mm machine guns. It would take more than the spinning slugs from the Kalashnikovs to do major damage, and Rockson wasn't about to wait around for the big guns to show up. He turned the plane suddenly, the back wheels skidding around with a screech. The moment the jet was aimed straight down the long takeoff path, Rock slammed the control wheel forward at the same time he pulled a lever by his side to full power.

The MIG jerked and rushed forward, shot like a ball from a cannon. He suddenly realized that he was going the wrong way as all the big yellow arrows painted on the concrete runway were pointing at him. But they'd just have to send the ticket via freefighters, Colorado, U.S.A. A jet tore down from the skies for a landing, a passenger flight, thank God, instead of another fighter. But seeing Rockson's MIG coming straight down its landing path, it veered sharply up and to the right.

"Almost there, pal, hang on," Rock yelled over the thundering roar of the engine. Archer had turned a ghostly shade of white and turned his head away from the curved glass of the cockpit cover, unable to look at the ground rushing faster and faster past him. Far ahead on the runway Rock suddenly saw a whole convoy of trucks being driven onto the airfield. Emergency and fire trucks were roaring toward him, bearing down from the opposite end of the field. The dial on the airspeed panel in front of him read two hundred thirty kilometers per hour. The jet felt like it wanted to rise. There was no time like the present. Wasn't that what Dr. Shecter always said? The lead vehicle trying to cut him off was a bright red fire truck, with soldiers hanging on for dear life on both sides. They fired at him with one arm, trying to get a clear shot at the jet, ready to die themselves to take out the humiliator of the Russian Empire. Rock pulled the wheel back as far as it would go, and the super jet shot up into the air at a forty-five degree angle, the wheels passing just inches over the heads of the firing troops. He couldn't hear their screams as the long jet exhaust flame reached out and burned the entire crew of the truck to a blistering mass of molten flesh.

Rock climbed and climbed into the sky, taking the jet up in as steep an angle as it could handle. Within a minute he was up into the slow-moving, mountainous clouds where he leveled off. Now what? He saw a small sign with a blinking purplish light below it reading Computer Assist and pressed the Enter button to the right of the screen.

What Course? The words flashed on a narrow six by twelve inch screen. Great—it wanted to help him, but how the hell did he answer the thing? The computer waited twenty seconds and then a second set of words appeared. *Instruction Sequence Mode—Push Button A-3.* Rock found and indented the nominated button, and almost instantly more words blinked onto the screen. *Use Keyboard*

Console Controls To Type In Instructions. Rock-son glanced frantically around for the Console Control Switch and at last found it. A keyboard about the size of a book popped out from the control panel and clicked into a horizontal position just in front of him. Rock typed in *Course America — USA — North.*

The computer digested the information and then spat out. *Airport?* Again he keyed in, hoping he could bluff the assist system. *No Airport — Special Mission — Top Security Clearance. Will Advise Later.* The computer again digested the somewhat strange information and then a green light blinked three times. *Course America — Await Advisement.* The jet shot forward, banking sharply to the left. They were on their way.

"Just sit back and enjoy the trip, hey Archer." But Archer wasn't enjoying it at all. He looked green around the gills, looking out the window at the clouds rushing past them and then, just as quickly straight ahead, trying to focus in on the back of Rock's seat and not to think too much about what was happening. Rock hoped the Russian Air Force supplied paper bags. The night grew clear after about ten minutes as the big puffs of moisture pressed ahead into the heartland of Mother Russia. Above them the stars twinkled like a billion billion eyes looking down on the strange planet Earth, a world of so much violence and death. Rock wondered if it was the same out there. Were there worlds where people loved instead of hated, where they evolved instead of tearing each other and their planet apart? Somewhere, somewhere out there in the infinite reaches of space, there must be at least one civilization that had learned to quench its violent instincts and produce rational beings. Perhaps creatures like the Glowers.

Suddenly an amber light sparked brilliantly to life directly in front of him. *Radar Picks Up 3 Fighters Locking In With Missile Tracking Equipment. Instructions?* Rock quickly typed in through the keyboard—*Options?*

The computer didn't hesitate this time. *Impossible To Destroy Enemy With Onboard Equipment.* Then it seemed to hesitate for a moment, as if unsure about questioning its controller and asked, *Why Is This Fighter Being Attacked By Craft Of The Russian Air Command?* Rockson gulped. He had lied to humans with some success in the past but a computer . . . He keyed in *Top Secret. Unauthorized Information For Any But Code Red Clearance. Direct Orders of Premier Vassily.* The computer again assimilated the data, its various command imperatives struggling furiously against one another, trying to sort things out. Rock looked at the radar screen. He could see the three small blips of the jets closing fast. They were a mere fifty miles away. Within a mile they would be within air-to-air missile range.

His eyes snapped back as the computer screen flashed on again. *Data Accepted. Evasion Mode Only Possible Method Of Nondestruction Of Craft.* Rock instantly typed in a command, his fingers dancing across the keyboard. *Carry Out Evade Mode.* The jet dropped from the sky like a stone, falling almost straight toward the earth, the nose pointing at the hard mountains far below. Behind him, Rock could hear Archer gurgling softly. His own stomach wasn't taking too kindly to the maneuvers. The MIG dropped for what seemed like an eternity until it at last leveled off a mere one hundred feet above the ground. Then it accelerated to nearly fifteen hundred miles per hour. Rock glanced out the cockpit window. He could see the vast Russian forests flying by below, mere blurs of gray. Every few seconds a reflection of some isolated village's lights would glint up and then just as quickly be gone. Sonic booms shook the ground behind them, leaving a trail of broken windows and fallen branches. Rock glanced back at the radar screen. The three MIGs in pursuit were breaking out of formation, each flying off in a different direction, searching for him. It had worked. They couldn't track the jet down so close to the ground, their radar unable to distinguish between the ground and moving piece of metal lost in the immensity of the solid earth below.

Rock took the breather to check his wound. His back ached painfully, but the blood flow seemed to have stopped. He could see a small swollen wound in the right side of his stomach as well. The slug had passed right through him. All the better. He didn't have to concern himself with taking it out. He keyed into the computer console. *Medical Supplies?* The computer immediately shot back with a long list of onboard medicines, bandages, drugs. Rock chose two — *Coagulant and Antibiotic Injections*. The memory took in the request, and then a small compartment swung open at the right side of the cockpit panel. A stainless steel tray containing two hypodermic needles filled with a thick, clear liquid whirred forward on rollers. Rockson took them out and emptied the load around the edges of the entry and exit wounds. Just as he finished injecting himself, he had the sudden paranoid thought that perhaps the computer was trying to poison him. But then grinned, realizing the absurdity of it. In a strange way one could trust machines: They wouldn't double-deal or stab you in the back. Man's best friend.

They flew for hours, the world below the MIG totally indecipherable to anything but the computer—just blurs and terrain melting together, moving by too fast for human perception. Occasionally, as they approached a mountain range or a towering forest, the jet would rise sharply and then just as suddenly drop down again to the lowest possible altitude.

Suddenly there was blue below them—flickering tips of waves and the glistening reflections of the galaxies of stars lapping at the top of the water's surface. *The ocean*, Rock realized. They were out of Russia, off the continent entirely. America lay ahead. The Doomsday Warrior felt himself slipping into unconsciousness. He hadn't slept for days. So much fighting and blood. At last his head leaned over onto his shoulder and he fell into a deep sleep. Archer's loud stuttering snores mixed with the roar of the jet's engines as they flew across thousands of miles of empty ocean.

Rockson was in a field of lillies, tall and white.

They moved slowly from side to side in a soft breeze. The sun was pure and yellow, sending down streams of soothing warmth. He heard a voice and turned—it was Kim, her golden hair falling softly around her silky shoulders. She rushed toward him and pressed her soft breasts against her chest. Together they dropped to the fertile earth and kissed softly. Robins and nightingales sang out sweet harmonies around them.

"Oh Rock," she whispered in his ear. "I love you so much."

"And I you," the Doomsday Warrior replied, his heart bursting with passion. He felt his soul opening like the soil itself to receive her love.

"Rock," she said again. "Rock, Rock, *Rock*." But the voice was growing louder, screaming in his ear until it hurt.

He awoke with a start and shook his head a few times until he remembered where he was—in the MIG. The dream disappeared like a ripple across a pond, though his heart ached to return to the fantasy. The computer screen was blinking, and an alarm was sounding over and over, shrill and frightening.

Fuel Is Nearly Gone—Fuel Is Nearly Gone— Fuel Is— Rock typed in *Can We Reach The United Soviet States?*

Destination Unclear. Possible To Reach Land. No Airfield Within Landing Possibility.

Make Land, he keyed in, and the alarm shut instantly off. He looked out the cockpit's curved glass. They were still above the ocean but close— close to home. He could feel it in his bones. Far off to the north the aurora borealis twisted in rainbow curtains of color, stretching off into myriad shades of blue and gold and violet. The magnetically excited light writhed in constantly shifting patterns of the most subtle gradation. But as the dawn sun broke behind them, the multi-colored waves slowly faded into the pale blue skies.

Suddenly Rock saw land ahead—America. How long had they been away? Weeks—months? It seemed like forever. An endless procession of enemies trying to destroy him. But he had survived yet again. The gods were still on his side, perhaps on America's side.

The computer alarm went off again and the screen lit up.

Fuel Remaining—Two Minutes. Ejection Process Beginning.

Ejection Instructions? Rock typed in.

Parachutes Below Front And Rear Seats. Push Button For Manual Release. Otherwise Ejection Will Occur Automatically At Moment Of Zero Fuel. The jet began slowly rising to three thousand feet, the minimum altitude for a jump.

Thanks Pal, Rock couldn't help but type in, wondering what the computer would make of it. But it remained silent, unable to digest the data. Rock leaned around in his pilot seat to wake Archer, but the Freefighter was already alert, staring back at him through sick-looking eyes.

"Time to leave," Rock said softly. He pulled out the parachute from beneath his seat and strapped it on around his back, showing Archer how to do the same. The big American became more and more concerned as he struggled with the straps, realizing what was about to happen.

"Noooo fall," he mumbled through tightly gritted teeth. "Archer nooo falllll."

"It's okay," Rock said soothingly. "These will take us down." He pointed to the chute on his back. Archer looked at the Doomsday Warrior with fearful eyes but continued strapping the chute on. He trusted Rock even though his heart beat rapidly, filled with unknown fears.

The MIG continued to rise, skimming just below some low-flying misty clouds. They passed the shoreline, and Rock could see the green and brown of the forests below. The morning sun rose higher into the sky, shedding a pure light on the jet and its occupants. Far off in the distance he glimpsed lakes — five of them — blue and sparkling. The Great Lakes — so they were up at the very northern border of the United States. It would be a long trek home, but the clear waters were a beautiful sight to his eyes.

Suddenly the warning alarm went off again. The computer flashed the words *Automatic Ejection — 10 Seconds*. Archer struggled furiously to get the front strap of his chute closed across his broad chest. The jet automatically slowed to two hundred miles per hour, and at the very instant that Archer snapped the locking mechanism closed, the cockpit covering flew off into the air above them. Their seats shot up and out of the falling plane. Rockson could hear Archer let out little yelps of fear as they flew out into the cold morning air.

Chapter Twenty-three

Thousands of miles away a group of creatures sat in a wide circle, their eyes shut tightly. They glowed with a blue sparkling electricity as their bodies pulsed with energy. They looked as if they had been turned inside out—their organ systems on the outside of their flesh—heart, kidneys, liver stomach, and brain all visible and pumping life through them. They called themselves only The People though they were known by another name to the human species: The Glowers.

They sat on small pillows, absolutely motionless. Their minds were linked together in an ever-changing pattern of thoughts and visions. They knew that Rockson was back. They could feel his energy as his body entered into the airspace of America. It was good. He was alive. They had not been sure he would survive when he had been taken away. Their powers of prophesy had been strangely clouded as if fate itself had been unsure what to do with him. But now he was returned to his land of birth—this man of ultimate destiny—Ted Rockson. But they could feel something else. A terror looming in the future—very near and very terrible. There was so much pain and blood in the vision they shared that they could barely stand to feel it. But they had to. That was their destiny—to see all, to know what would be. And only Rockson stood in the way of the darkness, the destruction. But they could not see beyond. Once again the future seemed uncertain as to its course. There was much possibility—for good—and for evil. It would be up to him. He alone could alter the time lines of mankind's future. But the darkness, the terror was strong. Very strong. They had never felt such a black energy, such evil. What the man Rockson was about to face would be the battle of his life, pitting the very elemental forces of the universe against one another—a war between the darkness and the light.

Chapter Twenty-four

Rockson fell slowly to the earth below. Above him he could see Archer's chute had opened as well, though the freefighter was kicking furiously as if trying to stay aloft through sheer leg power. The Doomsday Warrior looked down. The land spread out below him in all its crazy-quilt patterns of beauty and ugliness, life and disease. But it was his America. His country. And he had just struck a major blow against the Reds. Attacked them on their home ground for the first time in a century. And he had wounded them. The consciousness of just who was the strongest had tilted dramatically to one side on the changing scales of history. Things would be different now.

Rockson swung slowly back and forth in the wind as he fell lower and lower towards the fields of America.